Zimmermann
& Zimmermann

School, Trouble & True Love

Aus dem Deutschen
von Helena Ragg-Kirkby

Thienemann

“Julia,

I fell in love with you immediately! You’re so different from the other girls in the class. You’re so romantic.” Alex looks at me tenderly.

I smile back lovingly.

“Julia!” My mother’s voice **dragged** me back from my lovely daydream. “Aren’t you listening to a word I say?” She examined me **suspiciously**. “**There’s something the matter with you**. Are you **sickening for** something?”

I muttered something and wished that my family were a million miles away: my mother, who was just about to put her hand on my forehead – I’m almost fourteen, **for goodness’ sake**! – my father, who was giving me an equally concerned look, and my beloved little brother, whose spoon had just wandered into my pudding.

---

to drag – ziehen; suspiciously – verdächtig;
There’s something the matter with you. – Irgendetwas stimmt mit dir nicht.;
to be sickening for sth – an etw. erkranken;
for goodness’ sake – um Himmels willen

"Ow, that hurts!" he yelled as I gave him a kick in the **shins** under the table. My parents, of course, immediately had nothing more important to do than comfort their Timmi and to tell me that I, as his older sister, was **to make allowances for him**. The same old **stuff**, then.

I pushed my plate aside. "I'm not hungry any more," I said and stood up. Timmi pounced on my pudding with a shriek of **glee**.

"You have to eat, Julia, you're a growing girl!" cried Mum behind me as I made for the door.

Typical! The most important topic in this family is food. But there are other, far more fundamental things in life. Only nobody here has **realized** it yet, I thought angrily. I'd have loved to **slam** the door behind me. The fact that I could hear Mum and Dad **whispering** the word "puberty" was the only thing that stopped me from doing so.

With as much **dignity** as I could **muster**, I left the dining room. What I needed was a quiet place where I could lose myself in my thoughts. My thoughts of Alex. I smiled to myself.

---

shin – Schienbein;
to make allowances for sb – auf jmdn. Rücksicht nehmen;
stuff – Zeug;
glee – Entzücken, Begeisterung;
to realize – mitkriegen;
to slam – zuknallen;
to whisper – flüstern;
dignity – Würde;
to muster – versammeln

It all started two months ago. Our teacher introduced a new kid to our class who'd spent the last five years in America.

"Perhaps he speaks fluent English and can help us with our homework," said Hille, my best friend. "Then I could invite him to my Granny's house for a meal in return."

Her grandmother has a farm and really likes cooking, especially huge portions.

"I saw a programme on TV not long ago about fat Americans. D'you know, it's totally normal for people to be overweight there." She gave a small **sigh** and pulled her stomach in. "Oh well, whatever. Main thing is we've got someone to ask about our English tests."

But all thoughts of irrelevant things like tests were blown away when I saw Alex for the first time. This moment – I was one hundred percent certain of it – was one I'd never forget in my whole life! Never! Somehow the idea had **lodged** itself in the back of my mind that Alex Cleef would be a **chubby** boy with short hair and a dim **expression**, wearing a baseball cap on his head and an oversized sweatshirt with a stupid slogan. So I'd thought!

Instead, our teacher was followed into the classroom by this guy who could easily have been a member of the kind of boy band that everyone

---

sigh – Seufzer;
to lodge – festsetzen;
chubby – pummelig; expression – Miene

swoons over. And he'd have been the best-looking **of the lot**!

I **reckon** you could have **heard a pin drop** as Alex sat in the only empty seat in the classroom next to Oleg, who undoubtedly **failed** to appreciate just how lucky he was.

The boys all looked pretty **fed up**. It was clear to all of them that they **looked** pretty **old hat** compared to Alex. Or, to put it better, pretty **insignificant**.

At break most of the girls in the class immediately sprang into action. Jenny borrowed a bright red lipstick from her cousin in 10b and smeared it over her face. The colour, of course, didn't suit her in the slightest, but she acted pretty cool and was the first to speak to Alex.

"Huh," said Hille on the way home. "Jenny acts as if she were Supergirl or something."

I just nodded.

"That lipstick! And what's more, she's far too thin."

I nodded again. But all the same, Alex spent exactly seven minutes talking to her (I just happened to look at the clock). And despite the ridiculous lipstick!

---

to swoon – ohnmächtig werden;
of the lot – von allen; to reckon – glauben;
to hear a pin drop – eine Stecknadel fallen hören;
to fail – versäumen;
fed up – sauer;
to look old hat – alt aussehen (ugs.);
insignificant – unwichtig

Hille gave me a sidelong look. "What's the matter? You're not saying a word! So what do you think of the new boy?"

I said he was very nice, but that I wasn't particularly interested in him. Since my friend was still giving me suspicious looks, I added that I'd woken up horrendously early that morning so I was terribly tired. But, in fact, I was wide awake and just wanted some peace, even from Hille. I had to think – and think **big-style**.

During the following week it became clear to me relatively quickly that I'd fallen in love with Alex – just like all the other girls in the class. Except I didn't show it, unlike Eileen, who came to school hideously **tarted up** every day. Even Rita, who normally wore jeans and grey sweatshirts, had suddenly turned **fashion conscious**. Or, **at any rate**, she tried to be. Hille and I seemed to be the only ones who were still normal. When I cautiously asked Hille at one point whether she she might **fancy** Alex, too, she just laughed – but she didn't sound very cheerful.

"You surely don't believe I can compete with Eileen and all those girly girls," she said. "So it'd be a waste of time, wouldn't it?"

I had to agree with her really. Alex spent practically every break with Eileen or Jennifer and

---

big-style – gründlich;
to tart oneself up – sich auftakeln;
fashion conscious – modebewusst;
at any rate – auf jeden Fall; to fancy – mögen

seemed to be having a brilliant time. He did once sit with Ina from our parallel class in the schoolyard, but only for ten minutes. The next day, the class stars Eileen and Jenny were back in there. Alex didn't seem to want to waste his time on normal girls like Hille and me. In the end, I banned myself from thinking about him at all.

Unfortunately, it didn't work as I'd **imagined** it would. At any rate, I constantly dreamt about Alex – incredibly lovely dreams. Maybe it was because I mostly thought about him before I went to sleep, but he appeared pretty regularly in my dreams. And the greatest thing was this: in almost every dream he declared that he'd fallen in love with me right at the start.

I'd **snuggled** up in my **rocking chair** and was still lost in thought about Alex when there was a gentle knock on my bedroom door. Mum! She thinks she's being terribly **pedagogically sound** because she's been knocking on my door for a while now.

"I'm showing Julia that I respect her private sphere by doing it," she told a friend on the phone recently. "She's become terribly sensitive."

I decided to put Mum's pedagogical theories to the test. The second knock already sounded considerably more impatient, and when I still didn't

---

to imagine – sich vorstellen;
to snuggle – sich kuscheln;
rocking chair – Schaukelstuhl;
pedagogical – pädagogisch;
sound – gut, sicher

answer the third time, she just flung the door open.

"For heaven's sake, Julia, what's all this **nonsense** about? You can't just get up from the supper table, drop everything and disappear. And why are you sitting here in the dark?"

Mum switched the ceiling lights and my standard lamp on, and **scrutinized** me, frowning. "I don't like the circles under your eyes. Not enough sleep, or not enough fresh air, don't you think? Can't you go with Hille to her grandmother's farm again? Or do you know what? I've got an even better idea: let's go for a walk at the weekend! We'll have a nice lie-in first, a cosy breakfast, then we'll set off. You always used to enjoy that sort of thing. What do you reckon?"

I tried to grin, but didn't quite succeed. What were you supposed to say to a mother who thought that the black eye-liner that I'd **smeared** around my eyes just to try it out was black circles, and who suggested a day's walking with the family?

"Or are there problems at school?"

Dad had also appeared in the meantime. "Do you want me to help you a bit with your Maths again? For heaven's sake, Julia, you don't have to be a straight-**A student**! The main thing is that

---

nonsense – Unsinn;
to scrutinize – genau untersuchen;
to smear – schmieren;
an A student – ein Einserschüler

you pass. Right until she did her A levels your mother …"

"… got an E for Maths," I finished his sentence. I'd already heard that at least a thousand times, along with her miraculous rescue through consistent revision – and the sentence that Mum added, always with the same astonished smile, "It was really strange: I suddenly started to find Maths really good fun."

"I've not got any problems at all at school. Everything's going brilliantly," I reassured them both, wondering how I could get out of this situation as quickly as possible.

Mum had sat on my bed, and Dad was **leaning** on my desk. If he opens the drawer now, I thought – and I could hear my heart pounding – he'll see my **diary**, and he might find the key and open it at the right page and read what I dream about every night and …"

"You've got that strange look again," I heard Dad saying. Mum **shook her head**.

"You can't tell her how to look," she hissed. "Could you just go and see what Timmi's up to? He's suspiciously quiet."

It was obvious: she wanted to be alone with me. She probably hoped she'd be able to get more out of me that way. But I wasn't going to do her the favour. My first great love had nothing to do with

---

to lean – sich anlehnen;
diary – Tagebuch;
to shake your head – den Kopf schütteln

anyone but me. On top of that, it wasn't even a real love, more like virtual love or something. Whatever, I wasn't going to give Mum and her friends anything to **gossip about**.

Dad had got the message.

"Julia," he said, "you know that your parents are always here for you. You can always come to us if you've got a problem."

He went to the door, turned round again and seemed to be thinking. Then he said, "Good night, I'll go and check on Timmi."

Mum had moved an empty **wine gum** bag from under my bed with the tips of her toes and was now staring fixedly at it. "Well, then," she said finally. "I'm going to go, too. Don't forget that tomorrow's going to be a tiring day. There are lots of things on the agenda."

I hadn't the **faintest idea** what she **was on about**, but I nodded like a good girl.

"By the way," she said. "You wanted to have a big birthday party this year. Do you know yet who you'd like to invite?"

For a moment I was genuinely **baffled**. My mother normally regards birthday parties with complete horror. After Timmi's party with 12 friends from kindergarten on a rainy day, she'd **sworn** never to allow large numbers of birthday

---

to gossip about – über etw. lästern;
wine gum – Weingummi;
faintest idea – leiseste Schimmer;
to be on about sb/sth – über jmdn./etw. sprechen;
baffled – verwirrt; to swear – schwören

guests. And now this question about who I wanted to invite? What's more, my birthday was three months ago.

"We promised then that you could have a party in the summer," she said. "I reckon you could invite a couple of boys if you wanted."

It was all clear. Now I got it! She just wanted to know if I could be in love, and who with. But she'd have to wait a long time to find that one out. I had no desire to discuss my love life with my family.

"I'll see," I said. And then I couldn't stop myself from adding, "Perhaps I'll invite the whole class. There are 29 of us now!"

I could positively see Mum **give a start**. "There's still a little while to go," she said, and it sounded as if she wanted to **console herself**. "We'll talk about it again another day, okay?"

That night I dreamed about Alex again. This time we were standing under a tree. I was leaning against the trunk and it was swaying **to and fro**. Alex wanted to hold onto me, but I missed his hand. And then I woke up. Perhaps the dream had a deeper meaning? I absolutely had to find out I **resolved** as I stood in the bathroom **gazing** into the **mirror**.

The opportunity arose on the way to school.

---

to give a start – zusammenzucken;
to console oneself – sich selbst beruhigen;
to and fro – hin und zurück;
to resolve – entschließen;
to gaze – starren; mirror – Spiegel

Hille, it's true, was in an extremely **bad mood**, but I couldn't pay any attention to that.

"Why didn't you ring me back yesterday?" she wanted to know. "I told your brother three times that it was massively important. We're supposed to be translating that Martin Luther King text. The one with the dream and stuff."

I stopped right in the middle of the road. "Exactly," I said. "Hille, do you know anything about dreams?"

She **stared** at me. "Are you joking? You can't stay standing in the middle of the road just because we've not done our English homework." She dragged me to the edge of the road.

"I'm serious. I keep having really strange dreams, and I want to know what they mean."

My friend nodded slowly. "I see. My mother's got a book about it, but you probably wouldn't make anything of it. You're better off asking me. I know what dreams mean, you see. My grandmother told me once."

She cast a quick look around and lowered her voice. "She said that some people have a kind of second sight. And I reckon I've got it. D'you know, sometimes I dream that it'll rain the next day, and then it actually does rain. So when it comes to the weather forecast, I'm definitely just as good as the ones on TV. Sometimes I dream that I've messed up a test, and then that happens, too." She looked at her watch.

---

bad mood – schlechte Laune; to stare – anstarren

"Damn! If we don't get a move on, we'll get into trouble with Napoleon, too. Tell me your dream afterwards, then I'll tell you what it means. Okay?"

"Okay," I said, though I knew as I spoke that I'd never tell anyone my dreams. Not even Hille. It would be just too embarrassing.

We went into the classroom just before our history teacher. Alex was sitting in his place, looking so sweet that I almost had to shut my eyes for a moment. Why could I only ever dream about him? Why couldn't I look more like Eileen? Or at least go around being as self-confident as she was? And just talk to Alex? Instead of which ...

"He's assessing us for our **oral contribution**," I heard Hille whispering **indignantly**.

Napoleon – our history teacher had had this nickname for the last 120 years for sure – was holding an open notebook in his hand and was pointing his **index finger** in my direction.

"Julia!" he said after a short pause. "Now it's your turn to tell us something about the French Revolution." The nasty little man pointed to the clock. "Within the next couple of minutes, if you wouldn't mind."

I tried to remember something about the French Revolution, but failed. Why hadn't I at least put

---

oral contribution – mündliche Beteiligung;
indignantly – entrüstet;
index finger – Zeigefinger

my history book under my pillow last night? I had, in fact, intended to do some revision, but then I'd started thinking about Alex and …

"We didn't write anything down last lesson," I said rather lamely, but I knew full well it was pointless.

Napoleon smiled mildly. "You shouldn't have your knowledge in your exercise book: it should be in your little head."

I knew the **cliché**. He came out with it about three hundred times a year.

"I forgot we had History today," I mumbled.

Napoleon scrutinized me, shaking his head. "Other things on your mind, eh?" he said **mockingly**, producing his **biro** and writing my mark in his exercise book.

"Damn," whispered Hille next to me. "Now **he's bound to pick on** me."

She **hesitated** for a moment then jumped up. "Herr Dieringer, can I please leave the room? I feel terribly sick, I think I've …" She **stumbled** to the door with her hand over her mouth.

Napoleon watched her go, astonished. "I actually wanted to ask you what you know about the causes of the French Revolution!" he cried after her, but Hille had already **vanished**.

---

cliché – Klischee; mocking – spöttisch;
biro – Kuli;
he's bound to – er wird auf jeden Fall;
to pick on – es abgesehen haben auf;
to hesitate – zögern;
to stumble – stolpern; to vanish – verschwinden

Why didn't *I* think of that brilliant trick? I worked out my average in History on a piece of rough paper. Of course, only I could be that unlucky! With this magnificent oral contribution, I had exactly a C-minus. And I still needed a C to compensate for Chemistry. It was enough to make you **despair**.

Napoleon had found a new victim. As Benjamin knew precisely as little as I did, he finally repeated all the stuff from the last lesson himself.

Just to be on the safe side, Hille didn't reappear. She was **presumably** afraid that Napoleon would still test her in the last five minutes.

"We're doing group work today. After all, we have to keep up with the times even in History," I heard Napoleon saying at the front of the classroom. "Get together with your neighbour and work through pages 35 to 38 of your textbook. The questions on page 39 are your homework. Your *written* homework! Then our Julia will finally have something written in her book to **revise** from." A couple of **imbeciles** in the class giggled.

I fished Hille's History book out of her schoolbag and got down to work. How incredibly **thrilling** … *Discuss with your neighbour the possibilities open to King Louis XVI when …*

---

to despair – verzweifeln;
presumably – wahrscheinlich;
to revise – lernen;
imbecile – Idiot;
thrilling – spannend

"My dear Alex, this work **applies** to you, too," said Napoleon. I turned round curiously. Alex, who was sitting alone in the last seat, gave him a friendly smile.

"Oleg's not here, so I've not got a History book either."

"But ..."

"You said before that it was enough for one of us to have a book with them," Alex **interrupted** him.

I thought he was completely brilliant for saying that. He was so **self-assured**!

"He can have our book," suggested Benjamin.

"You've not finished, surely?" Napoleon's **eyes almost popped out of his head**. "You're supposed to do it thoroughly, not **make a botched job**."

He looked around, then **spotted** me. "Alex, come to the front and sit next to Julia. I'm quite sure Hille won't **dare** to come back for the rest of the lesson."

"No problem," said Alex. He stood up and **sauntered** to the front, to where I was sitting. And then he sat down next to me. Honestly, I was almost sick with sheer happiness! Alex, who I must have

---

to apply – betreffen;
to interrupt – unterbrechen;
self-assured – selbstbewusst;
his eyes almost popped out of his head – ihm fielen fast die Augen aus dem Kopf;
to make a botched job – rumpfuschen;
to spot – entdecken;
to dare – sich trauen; to saunter – schlendern

dreamed of a hundred times, was sitting next to me! Quite close. And if we were to look at the textbook together, we'd be even closer. I knew that this was **crunch time. Fingers crossed** that Hille wouldn't come back and **mess everything up**.

"So? What're we supposed to be doing?" Alex asked in a low voice after reading through the questions in the book.

He smelled faintly of soap, probably shaving foam. I'd have dearly loved to shut my eyes and soak up the scent, but I pulled myself together.

"We're supposed to discuss Louis XVI's possibilities," I said slowly, hoping that my voice wasn't trembling.

Eileen, who was sitting in front of me, turned round. "Do you need some help?" she asked, looking at Alex.

I shook my head. "We're doing fine," I **asserted** quickly. True, I hadn't got the faintest idea what we were supposed to be discussing, but I wasn't going to let this chance slip through my fingers.

Napoleon wandered from desk to desk, passing comment. "Read the pages through first," he suggested when he noticed that some people were already writing like mad. "Everything's in the textbook. All you have to do is read it, discuss it briefly,

---

to be crunch time – drauf ankommen;
fingers crossed – Daumen drücken;
to mess everything up – alles verderben;
to assert – sagen

and then write it out in your own words. It's not **rocket science**, is it?"

Alex grinned at me. "Okay then, let's read. What page?"

I pointed to page 35. We were sitting really close together.

"Finished?" he asked after a while and turned the page.

I nodded. I hadn't **taken in** a single word of what I'd read. Only one thing mattered: I was sitting next to Alex. I simply had to make something of it. I studied his profile **surreptitiously**. Alex really did look stunning. Someone said once that he could be in a film, and to my mind it was true. He was simply something special. All the boys in our class had short hair. Alex's hair was long. Sometimes he tied his black hair up into a **pony tail**. With anyone else it would have looked stupid, but it just suited him.

"D'you get what it's on about exactly?" he wanted to know.

"What?" I jumped. "Course I do, it's pretty **straightforward**."

He **shrugged his shoulders**. "Okay, if you think so. Do you think we'll manage to do the homework, too? I reckon it'd be great if we could get that done in class as well, don't you think?"

---

rocket science – Hexenwerk (ugs.);
to take in – begreifen;
surreptitiously – verstohlen;
pony tail – Pferdeschwanz; straightforward – einfach;
to shrug one's shoulders – die Schultern zucken

Suddenly everything became clear to me. Alex was at the very least just as clueless as me about History and the French Revolution. Obviously he was hoping that I'd answer the questions and that he could copy them from me. If I read those pages again, concentrating this time, I might be able to manage it, I thought. Perhaps Alex would sit next to me again now and then in the future. I'd have to find an **excuse** so that Hille would sit next to Oleg. I couldn't possibly tell her the truth.

"You can do the rest for homework. I'll mark it next time," said Napoleon. "We're finishing ten minutes early today. The **form leaders** have some more to tell you about the school party."

Then he packed his briefcase and disappeared. He didn't seem at all sorry to have to leave us ten minutes early. Any moment now Alex could stand up and go back to his place. And I'd have wasted my chance. Then Jenny turned round. She was smiling as if she was being photographed by a top photographer.

"Alex ..." she began.

Now I had to act. At once!

"Alex!" I heard myself whispering. "I've got the answers!"

He looked at me disbelievingly. "But you've still not written a single word."

"Could you possibly turn round again?" I **snapped** at Jenny.

---

excuse – Ausrede; form leader – Klassensprecher; to snap – fauchen

She looked quite astonished; rarely was I that unfriendly. But **I couldn't be doing with** witnesses for what I was about to say – and particularly not with Jenny.

"My brother had Napoleon for History a couple of years ago and he's kept his exercise books. I've just got to copy it from there."

Alex looked at me suspiciously. "And your brother passed History?"

"Of course," I assured him. "He always had As for it." But getting top marks wasn't the issue now. If I was lying, at least I was lying good and proper.

"If you're interested, I could give you the answers," I said. My voice **trembled** slightly.

But Alex didn't seem to notice anything. "Good idea," he said. "It'd be stupid to spend the whole afternoon racking my brains if you've got the right answers. Could you possibly fax them to me?"

Not like that, my dear boy, I thought.

"Wouldn't work," I said after a slight hesitation. "There's no way I'd get my brother's exercise book through the fax machine." We both laughed.

"But we could meet," I suggested. "What about around half four? At the old playground?"

Alex nodded. "Okay. And don't forget the homework." He stood up and returned to his seat.

When I turned towards him, he smiled at me. I could have **hugged** the whole world.

I can't be doing with sth – Ich kann etw. nicht gebrauchen;
to tremble – zittern; to hug – umarmen

I was pretty much in a daze for the rest of the morning. Perhaps it wasn't such a good idea after all to invent an older brother with an A in History. Quite soon I realized that I had no choice but to do the homework straight after lunch. And to do it as **thoroughly** as **befitted** a straight-A pupil.

After break I took my History book out of my desk, opened it at page 35 and slipped it into my Maths book. I'd better start work straight away.

"Hey, what's the matter with you?" asked Hille, who had reappeared at the start of the Maths lesson.

I smiled weakly.

"The F for History," surmised my friend. "Sorry I dropped you in it. If I hadn't run out of the room, I'd have been just as ..."

"Julia! Hiltrud! Could you two just be quiet!" Frau Frederici, our Maths teacher, was standing in front of us. She had that typical teacher's *aha-I've-caught-you-at-it* look on her face.

I tried to slip my History book out of the way, but it was too late. Frederici, of course, looked pretty astonished when she saw that I hadn't been hiding some **youth-corrupting** magazine in my Maths book but rather a school book.

"That doesn't belong in this class," she said lamely. "Concentrate on Maths instead – it's more useful to you."

---

thorough – gründlich;
to befit – sich ziemen;
youth-corrupting – jugendgefährdend

I finally got home shortly after two. I'd spent quite a long time wondering whether I should say "see you at four-thirty" to Alex on my way out. But then I'd decided against it after all. Hille might have become curious and if I knew her, she'd have been straight off to the playground with me. Of course, I'd have had to have **admitted** everything to her, and I didn't want to do that.

Mum had fetched Timmi from kindergarten and had got lunch ready.

"Julia," she called just as I was leaning my school rucksack against the **cloaks cupboard**. "I hope you've not forgotten that you've got to look after your brother this afternoon! You're best off playing with him. What about making models? A windmill, for example. Timmi ..."

I raced into the kitchen. "You can't be serious! I thought Timmi was going to kindergarten."

She laughed. "In theory, he is. But unfortunately the kindergarten teachers are on yet another training course today. The third one in four weeks, by the way." She thought for a moment. "Would you like a bit more **parsley** on your potatoes? And should I add the carrots straightaway?"

I looked at her uncomprehendingly, then shook my head. At that moment **I couldn't have cared less** what there was to eat. The only thing that interested me was that afternoon.

---

to admit – zugeben; cloaks cupboard – Garderobe;
parsley – Petersilie;
I couldn't have cared less – es war mir völlig egal

"Are you going to the **practice** this afternoon?" I asked.

She nodded. "Our new colleague is ill again. Well, with a bit of luck, I'll be back by quarter past four. Put the food in the oven, please; Timmi can **lay the table**. Give him a kiss from me!"

She **waved** to me, **grabbed** her bag and shopping basket and ran off. Perhaps, I **mused**, as I **shoved** the food into the oven and laid the table, Mum not being at home isn't that bad at all. Otherwise she'd want to know why I was suddenly getting changed and made up at lunchtime.

You see, the way I looked at the moment, I'd hardly **stand a chance** with Alex. **That** finally **dawned on me** when I examined myself in a department store mirror: faded jeans, **worn-out** sweatshirt – drab, all of it. No, I didn't, under any circumstances, want to turn up at the playground looking like that. I had to transform myself somehow by half four.

Alex would be **gobsmacked**; perhaps he'd say, "Julia, I'd never noticed how great you look." Or perhaps he wouldn't say it, but he'd think it all the

---

practice – Praxis;
to lay the table – den Tisch decken;
to wave – winken;
to grab – ergreifen;
to muse – grübeln;
to shove – schieben;
to stand any chance – eine Chance haben;
that dawned on me – es wurde mir klar;
worn-out – abgetragen;
gobsmacked – überrascht

same. There was just one **teeny weeny** problem: what should I put on? I stood in front of my wardrobe and stared gloomily into the chaos. Then I started to try on absolutely everything.

Of course, I just had everyday **gear** – nothing that would impress a dream guy like Alex. No short, **strapless** black dress, for example! I decided to ask for something like that the next chance I got.

But by half four I had to make do with whatever my wardrobe had to offer. I'd just decided half-heartedly on a red T-shirt with bright **beading** and a pair of three-quarter length white trousers when Timmi flung the door open and yelled that he was hungry.

Of course, the **pasta bake** in the oven had burnt slightly in the meantime, but my brother promised not to breathe a word to Mum. In return, I agreed to let him watch TV until four o'clock. Just to be on the safe side, I'd put my old things back on. You never knew with Timmi's table **manners**, and a **mark** on my white trousers would have been a catastrophe.

After lunch Timmi readily went into the living room with a **bar of chocolate** and switched the

---

teeny weeny – klein;
gear – Kleidung;
strapless – trägerlos;
beading – Perlenverzierung;
pasta bake – Nudel-Auflauf;
manners – Manieren;
mark – Fleck; bar of chocolate – Schokoriegel

TV on. Meanwhile I went through all the women's magazines that Mum had read in the last three months. It was a pretty big **pile**, but after quarter of an hour I'd found what I was looking for: a make-up "**on-test**" column headed: *Miraculously highlights your skin and gives you a glowing* ***complexion***. In addition there was a little perfume "on-test" headed *Aloha Garden*. That sounded interesting, and I hoped this **scent** would work on Alex.

The only thing that dampened my feeling of elation was that stupid History homework. For a moment I **toyed with** the idea of staking everything on my make-up and perfume and simply not taking the homework with me. I must have spent ten minutes chewing indecisively at a fingernail before deciding to take the work with me after all. **Better safe than sorry**! Stupidly enough, I still had to do it, though!

I looked at the clock and felt quite sick: it was already ten past three. I still hadn't got changed; I'd definitely need another half an hour for the homework, and meanwhile Timmi was watching a programme that my parents would never have allowed him to watch. But I couldn't **bother** about

---

pile – Haufen;
on-test – Pröbchen;
complexion – Gesichtsfarbe;
scent – Duft;
to toy with – mit etw. spielen;
Better safe than sorry. – Sicher ist sicher.;
to bother – sich kümmern

that now. I had more important things to do. After all, my entire life's happiness was **at stake**!

First off I decided to **treat myself** to the *Spa Treatment for Healthy, Shiny Hair* which my mother had bought and had left lying around in the bathroom. I applied the stuff to my dampened hair, wrapped a hand towel around it and got stuck into the French Revolution. In the meantime the hair spa could take effect, and I'd surprise Alex not only with my glowing complexion but my glossy hair as well.

The telephone rang. For one awful moment I feared he was ringing to cancel, but it was just Hille. We actually ring each other every afternoon even though we see each other at school all morning. And it's always good fun dissecting everything about school and going over everything again, but this afternoon it didn't suit me at all.

"I've got to look after my brother," I said. "You know that if you take your eyes off Timmi for a couple of minutes, **he's up to something**."

I promised to ring her that evening and then, ignoring Timmi's protests, turned the TV off and got back to my History homework. My supposed brother had an A in History; so I couldn't do my usual trick of **scrawling** any old thing in my book. I had to work carefully and I found it pretty diffi-

---

to be at stake – auf dem Spiel stehen;
to treat oneself – sich gönnen;
to be up to something – Blödsinn machen;
to scrawl – hinkritzeln

cult. For one thing, Timmi kept whining about wanting me to play Robber Hotzenplotz and the Grandmother. In this game I was always the grandmother whose **coffee grinder** is stolen. Timmi had **elaborated** upon the story slightly. At the end, I always end up tied to a kitchen chair begging for release. But at that moment I really wasn't up for it. I dragged my brother back to the TV, switched the children's channel on for him and was **reassured** to see that Peter Lustig was on. **Guaranteed** not to be dangerous!

I had just finished the second exercise – in **disguised** handwriting, naturally – when I heard loud hammering coming through the window, which was **ajar**. It was coming from the garage. I was just about to get **cross** about the noise when I got quite a shock. There was only one person who could be in the garage! The living room door was wide open and the TV was still on – but there was no sign of Timmi. I ran down the stairs. Timmi in the garage with Dad's tools – that could only go badly wrong.

I was pretty furious as I **wrenched** open the front door. What did my brother think he was playing at? Was I his nanny?

---

coffee grinder – Kaffeemühle;
to elaborate – weiter ausarbeiten;
reassured – beruhigt;
to guarantee – garantieren;
disguised – getarnt;
ajar – angelehnt;
cross – verärgert;
to wrench – reißen

By force of habit I closed the door carefully behind me. Ever since Timmi was born, my parents had been preaching at me about how he was the type to run off and that therefore all the doors had to be kept shut.

I ran into the garage. The hammering had stopped.

"Timmi, are you crazy? What's all this nonsense about?" I cried.

My brother was standing on a ladder with a **bucket** in one hand and was cheerfully throwing **soil** around.

"I'm having a carnival," he declared proudly. "There was a carnival on Peter Lustig."

I couldn't help laughing because he just looked so funny. Of course, that encouraged him no end, and he started to throw the soil at me.

"I'll tell Mum," I threatened. That didn't **impress** him in the slightest. He just laughed even more. Only when I threatened him with no TV for the whole of the next week did he stop.

"It was just a bit of fun," he said, climbing down the ladder. "Then I'll just play at garages again."

I took the hammer off him that he'd fetched from Dad's **tool bench** and looked severe. If only Mum would come home in good time and save me from this monster!

---

by force of habit – aus Gewohnheit;
bucket – Eimer; soil – Erde;
to impress – beeindrucken;
tool bench – Werkzeugbank

Timmi was already **wailing** again. "I want my pudding now, and then you've got to read to me! A ghost story. And then you'll be *really* scared."

"Huh," I said. He was in for a long wait. I had other problems now.

It was just before four. I had to wash the **hair spa** out, get changed, get made up, somehow do the last exercises and then shoot off. There's no way Alex would hang around waiting for me.

Timmi ran to the front door and pressed the bell. "I **need a wee**!" he cried. "Mum has to open the door quickly!"

I was about to ring the bell, too, when I felt boiling hot all over. "Oh, my God, Timmi, Mum isn't there! And the door's shut! What are we going to do now?"

Of course, I should have known. Little brothers **mess** everything **up** for you – and I really do mean everything. The only thing Timmi could do was press himself against me, **howling**, and wipe his snotty nose on my sweatshirt. Thank goodness I hadn't already got changed.

Was there a window open anywhere? An open patio door? No chance, guaranteed. Everything was shut on account of Timmi. So we two stood there, pretty much **at a loss**. If Mum got home in

---

to wail – weinen;
hair spa – Haarkur;
to need a wee – Pipi machen müssen;
to mess up – verderben;
to howl – heulen;
at a loss – fassungslos

time, I could still get changed. But what about the hair spa on my head? I could have howled with **rage**.

The phone rang in the house. Dear God, I prayed, don't let that be Mum ringing to tell us that she's got to work late.

Timmi had calmed down meanwhile. "Do we have to sleep outside?" he asked. "And Mum and Dad, too?"

I didn't reply. I knew for a fact that Mum had hidden a key somewhere for such emergencies. But where? Typical that nobody had told me where I'd find it. But for years now everything in our house had just **revolved** around Timmi. I **scoured** the front garden, turning over every large stone in my search for a key. The church nearby struck quarter past four.

Something had to happen now, or I could write Alex off. Hair washing, getting changed, make up – if I hurried, I might be able to manage it in ten, twelve minutes. It took five minutes to get to the playground by bike. And I could expect Alex to wait five minutes. After all, he was getting something in return.

"Listen, Timmi!" I knelt down beside him and looked severely at him. "I've just got to **nip out**. Wait here until Mum or I get back, okay? And don't move a millimetre from the door. Got it?"

---

rage – Wut; to revolve – drehen;
to scour – absuchen;
to nip out – kurz rausgehen

It had occurred to me that the bathroom window was ajar. With a bit of luck and a long ladder, I might be able to open it. Of course, Timmi blubbered a bit, wanting to know what he was supposed to do if robbers came and all that sort of nonsense.

"They'll take you with them if you don't shut up!" I yelled at him. I was just on the point of losing it. I impressed upon him yet again that he mustn't move from that spot under any circumstances, and then I fetched the ladder from the garage.

When he saw me, my brother, of course, **freaked out** and cried that he wanted to climb the ladder as well. I just gave him a cold smile.

"Fourteen-day TV ban."

Timmi didn't say another word.

The ladder was too short, but nothing could stop me now. I wanted to meet Alex; I was **hell-bent** on it. All the other girls had tried in vain. He didn't have time for anyone in the afternoons. Someone once said they'd seen him at the cinema with Lisa from our parallel class, but that turned out to be just a rumour. I, Julia Martin, would manage it. I would meet Alex today!

I made my way up over a projecting section of wall. I pushed the window open, climbed in, and dropped down onto the bathroom carpet. I got up, looked in the mirror and let out a shriek. Alex

---

to freak out – durchdrehen;
hell-bent – wild entschlossen

would probably have to wait longer than five minutes for me. I shook the soil, which was stuck to the remainder of the hair spa, into the wash basin. I'd worry about the rest later on.

First of all I had to fetch Timmi and stick him in front of the TV. Mum would complain when she got home, but I didn't care now. Then I'd get my appearance into enough order to stop Alex being too **thunderstruck**.

I ran down the stairs and **flung** open the door.

---

to be thunderstruck – wie vom Donner gerührt sein;
to fling – reißen

"Hello Julia,"

said Jenny, giving me a cheerful grin. Alex, leaning nonchalantly against the house wall, grinned, too. The only one not grinning was me.

"I bumped into Jenny on the way and told her everything. She said there was no need for you to make a special trip to the playground. I mean, you ..." He started to stammer. I didn't say a word.

"We thought we'd just drop by and fetch the History homework," she piped up. She'd recently done her **dyed** jet-black hair into **loads of** little **plaits** and looked pretty **ludicrous**. And the looks she was giving Alex! Simply **ridiculous**!

"Are we early? Are we **disturbing** you?" she asked me.

---

to dye – färben;
loads of – viele;
plait – Zopf;
ludicrous – albern;
ridiculous – lächerlich;
to disturb – stören

We, we! Jenny was acting as if she and Alex belonged together.

A dark blue car turned into our driveway. Mum, totally stressed out yet again, got out and heaved her shopping basket off the back seat.

"Sorry, we still had three patients and then I had to do a bit of shopping, and ..." she stared at me, horrified. "Julia, look at the state of you! Has something happened? Is something wrong with Timmi?"

He, meanwhile, had discovered a bar of chocolate in the shopping basket and was whining about wanting to eat it right away.

"Welcome to the madhouse," murmured Mum, pushing him into the house. "Do you all want to come in, too?"

I shook my head. A conversation between Alex and my mother about my invented brother was all I needed. Alex had **retreated** a couple of steps and was acting as if he were desperately interested in our front garden. He seemed to feel somewhat uncomfortable. He probably felt bad because he'd dragged Jenny along with him.

"So what are we going to do now?" he asked. He tried to smile, and I found him so incredibly **gorgeous** that I almost gasped. Jenny just gave a stupid giggle.

"We'll wait until Julia is with it again and gives us the homework. What do you reckon?"

---

to retreat – zurücktreten;
gorgeous – hinreißend

I could have **strangled** her, the false cow. A hundred percent certain she'd heard something about our meeting and had then "just happened" to bump into Alex. Prior to that, though, she'd sloshed at least half a litre of perfume over herself and had got her hands on her mother's lipstick. And the stretchy floral skirt was sure to belong to her older sister; there were **pleats** where there weren't supposed to be any. To my mind, Jenny looked simply ridiculous.

"... the homework," said Alex, still smiling.

I pulled myself together. "I'm so sorry, but I've not **got round to** looking for the book yet," I said. "I did a bit of **gardening** and completely forgot that you wanted to meet me, Alex."

That hit home. Jenny swallowed. "It doesn't matter," she murmured. "History's not that important."

Alex gave me a pleading look. "We've not got Napoleon again until the day after tomorrow. Could you possibly bring the book into school tomorrow? That would be just great of you."

All I could do was **nod**. I'd been totally **smitten**. I'd fallen completely in love with Alex.

"Great," said Jenny, taking his hand. "Then let's go, what do you think?" She turned round again.

---

to strangle – erwürgen;
pleat – Falte;
to get round to – dazu kommen; gardening – Gartenarbeit;
That hit home. – Das saß.;
to nod – nicken;
to be smitten – total hingerissen sein von jmdm.

"I didn't know you were into gardening. Do you choose to do it or do your parents make you?"

I was sure that Alex would have liked to sink into the ground, but Jenny, of course, didn't notice a thing. She's as sensitive as a **sledgehammer**. Alex gave me an **apologetic** wave, then disappeared in Jenny's wake.

I was still standing by the door when Mum **emerged** to heave the **crates** of mineral water out of the **boot**. She was initially about to complain, but when she saw my face, she smiled gently. "Hey, Julia, have you by any chance **fallen for** him?"

I used my **sleeve** to wipe the tears from my face. "No, I haven't!" I lied. "They were just two kids from my class and ..."

"I understand," Mum nodded. "Julia, we can be quite open with one another. It's completely normal to fall in love at your age. And sometimes you can be unhappily in love, too. Just think, when I was fourteen ..."

I could have screamed.

I didn't have the slightest **desire** to hear stories from Mum's youth. This was *my* life, and she had no right ...

---

sledgehammer – Vorschlaghammer;
apologetic – entschuldigend;
to emerge – rauskommen;
crate – Kiste;
boot – Kofferraum;
to fall for – sich verlieben;
sleeve – Ärmel;
desire – Lust

"Julia's in love, Julia's in love," sang Timmi from the top of the stairs. I ran upstairs, past him, and into my bedroom.

"Mum, who's Julia in love with?" I heard him asking.

I threw myself onto my bed and resolved never to be like Mum when I grew up. And never to have a child like Timmi.

Things carried on in the same way over supper. Timmi thought it was incredibly funny to keep saying that I was in love. I finally had to take action before the whole neighbourhood knew about it!

"I got an F for History today," I said gloomily. "You know what that means, of course."

Mum and Dad just looked at one another.

"Those two from my class who were here this lunchtime in fact wanted to revise with me, but ..." I thought quickly. Timmi was just about to say something else **inappropriate** when it **struck** me. I pointed my index finger at him. "He was so stupid with his **messing about** that they didn't want to any more and went home."

I got up and simply ignored Timmi's howling. I had, you see, just come up with a brilliant idea.

"But I've still got a chance in History," I said. My

---

inappropriate – unpassend;
to strike – einfallen;
to mess about – herumalbern;
expectantly – erwartungsvoll

parents looked at me **expectantly**. "Napoleon's going to give us a mark for our next homework. If I get an A, that'd be enough to give me a C in History, and then I won't have to repeat the year. Maybe one of you could help me a bit this evening. I could just bring my History book down."

I spent the rest of the evening trying to ring Hille while Mum was finishing my History homework. I absolutely had to tell someone about Jenny's ludicrous **behaviour**. Hille would definitely understand. She's totally different from me. Much more practical and robust, according to my mother. Hiltrud doesn't let things get to her so easily. Perhaps that's why Hille and I have been friends since **primary school**. Hille always has a solution to everything. To almost everything. When she was madly in love with Stefan Patschke two years ago, she just went up to him in the schoolyard and asked him to go out with her.

Stefan was so gobsmacked that he immediately said "yes" out of shock. But Hille realized in time that he wasn't that great after all, and since then she's been pretty **fed up** with boys. Or so she says, anyway.

I must have tried her number ten times, but nobody answered. I sat down at my desk and stared at my English book. I'd worked out a couple of

---

behaviour – Verhalten;
primary school – Grundschule;
to be fed up – es satt haben

weeks ago that if I revised ten words of vocab every day, I could ask to have a quick oral vocab test just before the end of the school year and might be able to **balance** things up a bit. But, unfortunately, I hadn't revised ten words every day! I'd mostly sat at my desk thinking about Alex.

For sure, Jenny had absolutely **forced** herself upon him this afternoon. It had been quite obvious that he'd found her behaviour embarrassing. Maybe it had opened his eyes and ...

Stop! said a **malevolent** voice inside me. If he thinks she's so stupid, why did he go with her when she took his hand? He could have said, "Hey, Jenny, I want to visit Julia. I'm staying here." But he hadn't. But he'd looked so sweet, as if he wanted to ask forgiveness for everything. Perhaps ...

"Julia!" Mum **tore** me **out** of my **reverie**. This time she'd come into my room without knocking. "Oh, you're doing English! I don't want to disturb you. Here's your History homework. If you don't get an A, then I don't know why. You've just got to copy it out, okay?" She handed me two densely written pages.

"Amazing!" I cried. "Do you still know that much about the French Revolution?"

Mum laughed. "I rang Frau Bergmann's daugh-

---

to balance – ausgleichen;
to force – zwingen;
malevolent – böswillig;
to tear out – herausreißen;
reverie – Träumerei

ter. Ulrike! You still remember her, don't you? She's studying History and something else in Berlin and was pleased to hear from us again. If I'd written down everything she said on the topic, you'd have been able to hand in an entire book to Herr Dieringer. If you've got any more questions, you can just give her a ring."

"Thanks, Mum!" I hugged her. She, of course, had no idea how much she'd helped me. Alex wouldn't believe it.

"Something's wrong with you," said Hille when she called for me the next day. "Are you still worried about Napoleon? It really was mean of him to give you an F."

I shook my head. "Nah, I've already got over the F. And anyway, he promised to give us a mark for the homework, and that's guaranteed to make up for the F. But I feel a bit sick. I think I might have **stuffed myself** with too much chocolate yesterday."

Hille nodded understandingly. She's pretty overweight, and entirely because of all the sweet things she stuffs herself with. She may keep saying it's because she's got such heavy bones, but I reckon even she doesn't really believe that.

I preferred not to tell her anything about my unhappy love for Alex. Firstly I was afraid she'd laugh at me. "Everyone fancies him. Can't you think of anyone else?" she'd probably say. And secondly I

---

to stuff oneself – sich voll stopfen

had a stupid feeling that I'd somehow **desecrate** my feelings if I talked about them. At any rate so long as everything was so unclear between him and me.

I might have had a superb History homework, but I still had no idea how to present it to Alex. Just going up to him and putting the two sheets on the table was stupid. And I didn't dare either. But I didn't want to tell Hille any of that. Far better **to fob her off** with sickness.

We were just standing at the bus stop when a blue car stopped beside us and Dad wound the window down. "I've got to take Timmi to kindergarten. **Do you want a lift** part of the way?"

"Why didn't you say earlier that you were going?"

Dad just laughed. "Sorry, but you left the house so quickly. Anyway, it may be that you two would rather be left in peace to catch the bus."

"No way!" Hille rolled her eyes. "You don't get a seat on the bus in the mornings – all you get is in a bad mood. **Budge** up a bit." She squashed in next to Timmi, who had **spread** his entire cuddly zoo across the back seat and immediately attacked her with a tiger.

I turned to her. "In the car, however, sitting next to my dear brother, you only ever feel in the best of moods!"

---

to desecrate – entweihen;
to fob sb off – jmdn. mit etw. abspeisen;
Do you want a lift? – Willst du mitfahren?;
to budge – sich rühren; to spread – ausbreiten

Hille just laughed.

"Hey, Hille!" Timmi's poisonous green crocodile snapped in front of her face. "Julia's in love."

I could have boxed his ears.

Dad said **soothingly**, "My dear Tim, just **put a sock in it** and stop constantly **getting at** your big sister."

Of course, Timmi had to **make** yet another big **fuss** and did actually put a sock in his mouth.

Hille shook him. "Hey, Timmi, you can take it out again." I must have given a half audible sigh as Dad gave me a sidelong look. Mum had obviously told him what she **suspected**: that I was unhappily in love, and had asked him **to treat me with kid gloves**.

"I'll take you to school first," he said. "Timmi's kindergarten can wait a little while."

If it had made Hille curious, she didn't show it. The whole morning she acted as if nothing had happened. But I had the feeling that everybody could tell how much in love I was just by looking at me.

Alex had overslept and didn't appear until the third lesson. I felt my heart pounding as he made

---

soothingly – beruhigend;
to put a sock in it – den Mund halten;
to get at – anpflaumen;
to make a fuss – einen Wirbel machen um;
to suspect – den Verdacht haben;
to treat sb with kid gloves – jmdn. wie ein rohes Ei behandeln

his way past me to his seat. Just at that moment, Frau Faulhaber-Enderlein, our French teacher, picked on me. Normally I didn't have any problems with translating, or at least not any particularly big ones. But I just couldn't do it. I simply couldn't come up with a single clear thought. All I had going round my head was "Alex" and "should I just go up to him at the next break and put my homework down on his desk?"

Frau Faulhaber-Enderlein was still waiting for my translation. I wouldn't have been surprised if she'd said, "Julia, am I mistaken, or are you in love?"

I tried to concentrate and did manage to translate about a third of the sentence until I was stopped by Hille clearing her throat nervously at the side of me. Faulhaber-Enderlein gave me a meaningful look and finally said that some people needed to learn their vocab more thoroughly. Then she picked on Eileen who translated three sentences **effortlessly**. No wonder – she didn't have the problems I had.

I looked at the clock. Still twenty minutes to go before the main break. On the one hand, I could hardly wait; on the other hand, I was pretty scared about it. Would someone make a stupid remark if I gave Alex the homework? Maybe he'd just say "thanks" and that'd be it, I mused. I **sighed** gently.

---

effortlessly – mühelos;
to sigh – seufzen

Hille gave me a sidelong look. "Don't worry, everything'll be fine."

I looked at her, astonished. Could Hille read my thoughts?

"Faulhaber won't give you a mark for that," she whispered to me. "She's not as mean as Napoleon."

I nodded. It was better not to tell Hille about my problem. There's no way that girls like Hille, who just go up to boys in the schoolyard and tell them that they like them, could understand my problem. I'd never manage to casually arrange to meet Alex. Instead, I'd stammer out something **daft** or I'd stuff my exercise book into his hand without saying a word.

I must have sighed again because Hille gave me a warning nudge. "Faulhaber's watching," she whispered. "Come on, turn over – we're on the next page."

The bell went for break and I took a deep breath. I'd stand up in a minute and act as if I'd just remembered the business about the History homework. Then I'd give Alex a friendly wave and …

"I'll just dictate to you what you absolutely have to revise for the test the day after tomorrow," said Faulhaber, searching in her **shabby** brown briefcase for some photocopies or another that she urgently had to hand out.

---

daft – blöd;
shabby – schäbig

A couple of boys **grumbled** loudly that they really couldn't take in anything else now, and that it was break anyway.

"We've got a right to free time, too!" cried Jonas. His voice squeaked as he said it, and everyone laughed.

By now, my History book was lying under my French book on the desk. I had a new plan. Alex wanted the homework from me, that was for sure. If he went out at break, he'd have to pass me. I'd then just quickly ask him, "Do you want it?" and hold the book out to him.

That was, I thought, not bad for starters. Then, of course, he would have to give me the homework back, and that would definitely be the opportunity for something to happen. Or I could ring him in the afternoon and remind him that he absolutely had to bring the book with him the next day. It'd all be much easier on the phone.

Faulhaber dictated at least three grammar chapters to us that we had to revise. Hille wrote it all down **assiduously**. "Oof," she said finally. "If she's really planning to include everything she's listed, I'll be spending the next three days revising non-stop. It's not right." She laughed shortly. "So I might as well not bother. Shall we go outside?"

I shook my head. I turned round **deliberately inconspicuously**. Alex was still sitting in his seat,

---

to grumble – klagen;
assiduously – eifrig;
deliberately – mit Absicht; inconspicuously – unauffällig

writing. He was presumably busy doing his homework for the next class.

Hille examined me thoughtfully. "I need to buy something to eat." She opened her snack box. "**Radishes**. Yuck. I knew it, the moment my mother ..."

Alex had got up and was **rummaging** in his school bag.

Hille looked at me expectantly. "You coming now?"

"I've just told you that I'm staying in the classroom!" I snapped at her.

She gave a start. "Wow, aren't you ever in a bad mood. Well, see you later then."

I turned my head briefly. Alex had got a can of mineral water out of his bag and was coming towards me.

"Alex, oh, by the way ..." That was *my* voice that sounded so **croaky**.

"Alex!" Eileen was standing at the classroom door, beaming. "Jenny asked her parents. It's all go for the party. You coming outside with us for break?"

I sat there holding the superb History homework, done to the highest possible standard by my mother and a third-year History student. I could have **wept** as he disappeared with Eileen.

---

radish – Radieschen;
to rummage – wühlen;
croaky – krächzend;
to weep – weinen

"Alex?!" Hille had sat down next to me.

There was no point **denying** it. Hille had spent the first five years of her life living with her grandparents on a farm before her mother had re-married and taken her to live with her. Thanks to her time on the farm, my friend has an unfailing **sense** for everything. "I knew days in advance when a **calf** was about to be born. Or that an animal didn't have very long to live," she'd told me a while ago. "My grandmother always said that nothing remains a **secret** from me."

In any case, my friend had clearly realized what was wrong with me. I looked around. There was nobody in the classroom but us. I nodded.

"Oof," said Hille for the second time that day. She looked at me half sympathetically and half admiringly. "Well, that's a nice plan you've **come up with** there!"

I tried to grin. "'Come up with' sounds good. But, in fact, it only came about because you ran out of the room in History yesterday. Napoleon sat him next to me, and I suddenly realized that I liked him. Liked him a *lot*, to be honest." Never in a million years would I have admitted that I'd been in love with Alex for ages. I wouldn't admit that even to Hille.

"The competition's tough," asserted my friend

---

to deny – abstreiten;
sense – Sinn;
calf – Kalb;
secret – Geheimnis;
to come up with – sich ausdenken

after a while. "Hey, don't you want your sandwich?"

I pushed my cheese sandwich over to her and shook my head.

"What do you mean, 'competition'? D'you think I *chose* Alex?" I felt the tears well up. "Hille, it's so stupid. I always thought being in love was nice. But at the moment I just feel **rotten**. I was just smitten, you know? Of course, I know that everyone fancies Alex. You, too?"

She took an extra large bite of my cheese sandwich and chewed it slowly. "I do a bit," she admitted after a moment's hesitation. "But to do you a favour, I'll **renounce** him right away. We're friends after all."

She smiled at me, and for a moment I felt bad for not having told her about my feelings for Alex.

She shook her head. "Anyway, I've got other problems at the moment. How to get through this school year, for instance. And how I'm finally going to get a holiday job that pays well."

I nodded sympathetically. "What's going on with your **applications**? Alfa Phone and stuff?"

"**Useless**, completely useless!" Hille shoved the remainder of my bread angrily into her mouth. "I had an interview yesterday evening. God, they make such a song and dance about it, it's as if you

---

rotten – furchtbar;
to renounce – verzichten auf;
application – Bewerbung;
useless – sinnlos

were applying for a post for life. And all I want is a job for four weeks of the summer holidays."

"So it didn't go very well?"

She laughed mockingly. "Didn't go very well – ha! Nicely put. D'you know what I had to do?" She rolled her eyes. "I had **to dress up** as a **mobile** and go round the **pedestrian precinct** handing out **leaflets** ..."

"As a mobile? You're joking!"

"Unfortunately not! As a mobile! Bright green! In this funny plastic case! But it only turned really bad when I had to answer nothing but stupid questions. Why kids need mobiles and stuff. I couldn't think of a single answer. Can you imagine me being totally lost for words?" She took a deep breath. "At any rate, I shan't be spending the summer holidays in a **garish** green plastic case. So that's a **consolation**."

"What now?"

She tried to grin, but it was pretty unsuccessful. "I've still got three applications on the go, and I'm pretty **keen on** one of them. *ModeMed* in Eisenbahnstrasse. That's something respectable, so my mother says. I've heard that you can get the stuff that doesn't sell very well for peanuts if you work

---

to dress up – sich verkleiden;
mobile – Handy;
pedestrian precinct – Fußgängerzone;
leaflet – Flugblatt;
garish – grell;
consolation – Trost;
to be keen on – scharf darauf sein

there. I wouldn't mind that." She sighed. "But my chances are probably **zilch** there, too."

"But you're normally so ..." I thought briefly, "... so self-confident. To just act with Napoleon as if you were feeling sick and then to spend the whole lesson outside. I'd never have dared."

"That wasn't a problem. I had nothing more to lose. Napoleon knows one way or the other that I don't get History. I just didn't want to hear the usual 'well, you need to do some revision for once, my dear Hiltrud'. But the holiday job – that's different. There's something at stake."

I had to laugh. "I'll apply for you, and you can sort out the Alex business in return."

We were both still giggling as the classroom gradually started to fill up ready for the next lesson. Only when I saw Alex with Jenny in tow, did I stop giggling.

The next few days were very dreary: three tests and, on top of that, our sports day was **cancelled**, when I'd been so looking forward to it! At least it would have meant missing two Maths lessons.

On top of that, Timmi's kindergarten was closed because of suspected **headlice**, and my brother was at home all day. It was just unbearable.

There was just one small **ray of light**: Jenny

---

zilch – gleich null, rein gar nichts;
to cancel – absagen;
headlice – Kopfläuse;
ray of light – Hoffnungsschimmer

seemed to be ill. Hille suspected that the heap of tests could have brought on her illness. Whatever the case, my path would have been free, purely theoretically speaking. I could have gone up to Alex at break and flirted with him a bit, then arranged to meet him in the afternoon ...

Well, that was the theory. Instead, I waited **in vain** for him to talk to me about the History homework. But he seemed to have forgotten it, just like Napoleon, who didn't give a moment's thought to collecting in our History books.

On the second day, directly after the Maths test, Hille dragged me into the yard.

"You've got to do something, or nothing will happen. And Jenny can't get in your way at the moment, so you've got to make the most of it," she'd said to me at least three times on the phone.

Of course, I knew she was right. I didn't actually believe in the **fairytale prince** who suddenly drops out of the sky any more.

"The yard is exactly the right place," she said. "No one will notice if you talk to him."

Somehow Hille managed to stand right next to Alex at the main break. I moved discreetly next to the pair of them. She gave him a friendly punch in the side.

"So, did you **muck** that test **up** as well?"

He grinned feebly. "I discovered my own kinds

---

in vain – vergeblich;
fairytale prince – Märchenprinz;
to muck up – vermurksen

of arithmetic. They probably don't quite match up with the ones in the text books that Frederici uses for Maths."

"Main thing is you get the right answer," I heard myself saying. Alex looked at me briefly, then nodded.

Hille winked at me. "You've just got to start talking," she'd impressed upon me in the classroom. "Just be completely normal, **slag** school **off** a bit and stuff. Then I'll suggest we all agree to meet this afternoon to revise, and for some reason or another I then can't make it. What d'you reckon?" Brilliant idea, Hille, I'd said – and I'd felt great when I was still upstairs in the classroom.

But now, in the yard, directly opposite Alex, yet again I couldn't construct a single sensible sentence. To my mind, everything I said sounded incredibly **limp** and unimportant. And I'd had so much to tell him.

"We're going to do a bit of Physics revision this afternoon," said Hille. "What do you think to ..."

"Well, young man!" The **caretaker** tapped Alex on the shoulder, looking angry. "Now I've finally caught you!"

Alex turned round. "What? Who've you caught? I ..."

The caretaker shook his head. "That **chewing gum** on the stairs was yours. You dropped it this

---

to slag off – schimpfen auf;
limp – lahm; caretaker – Hausmeister;
chewing gum – Kaugummi

morning; someone saw you. You're coming with me here and now, my friend, and scraping it off, or there'll be big trouble."

Alex protested a bit, but it made no difference.

"What do you reckon to revising Physics with us?" Hille called after him, but he was already **out of earshot**.

"Oh, wow," she said to me. "I'm afraid we've got a lot of work on our hands."

---

out of earshot – außer Hörweite

"By the way,"

said Hille as she **fiddled around**, trying to **mend** the broken drawer of my desk, "Do you know that Jenny's having a summer party?"

"Stop **wobbling**," I murmured. I looked up only briefly. "If we can't work out the next exercise, I'll **have a fit**. Why doesn't it work? I've changed the formula around properly, for goodness' sake – or have I miscalculated? Just *look*, would you?" But Hille had already given up.

"D'you know that Alex is the only boy in the whole class who she's invited?" Hille scratched little figures on her sheet of paper and looked at me. "D'you notice anything?"

I nodded. "Of course I do, I'm not blind. And Eileen's friends with Jenny, and she's totally **mad** about Alex. But Jenny probably stands a better

---

to fiddle around – herumspielen; to mend – reparieren;
to wobble – wackeln;
to have a fit – die Krise kriegen; mad – verrückt

chance. The way she carries on! D'you think he's in love with her?"

Hille thought for a moment. "No, I don't think so. I reckon that he always comes when she calls, and he fetches her drinks and stuff. But he's definitely not that into her. And, of course, he hasn't said he'll go to her summer party yet."

"How do you know all that?"

"Seventh sense!" She laughed loudly. "No, seriously, I met half the class on the way home. To be honest, it was just Carlo and Julian, and I think they were both pretty fed up that they weren't invited. Julian was at any rate; after all, he was sort of half **going out with** Eileen at one point."

"If Alex hasn't said he'll go to the party, then ..."

"... then there could be all kinds of reasons for it," my friend interrupted me.

"Then I have a chance, purely theoretically at least," I said, ignoring her objections. "All I'd have to do is just give him the chance to get to know me. Maybe he'll fall in love with me then. I mean, I don't look all that bad either."

My friend looked me up and down. "Nah, you really don't look that bad."

Afterwards I was annoyed by what she'd said. I thought I looked quite good, in fact. Better than **overweight** Hille, at any rate. And my long hair suited me well, or at least Mum said so. But that wasn't much help if I didn't dare to speak to Alex.

---

to go out with sb – mit jmdm. befreundet sein;
overweight – übergewichtig

The Physics test was just great! If I'd revised yesterday instead of talking to Hille about Alex, it would, of course, have been manageable, but as it was ... It was the same for Hille. She kept giving me despairing looks, but I just shook my head. If she'd been counting on my help, she'd miscalculated. I knew just as little as she did.

"Still three classes to go," she **moaned** after we'd all handed our work in. "And two of them are German. Goodness knows how I'm supposed to survive. And then another interview this afternoon."

I nodded, but my thoughts were elsewhere. With Alex, naturally. I dreamed about him again last night. I don't remember exactly what happened in the dream, but the very thought that Alex appeared in my dreams made me happy. That was why I'd been in a good mood up until breakfast. But by the time Timmi had tipped his cocoa over my white jeans, the mood had definitely been ruined. I'd yelled at Timmi and he'd gone running off howling to Mum, and I'd had to suffer all the usual stuff: "You're the older sister ... find it very disappointing ..."

I'd put my jeans straight into the washing machine on a 90-**degree** wash, but I wasn't sure that the horrible marks really would come out.

"Hey, Julia, you're not listening to a word I say!" complained Hille.

---

to moan – stöhnen;
degree – Grad

"Yes, I am. I heard you clearly," I said. I pushed over to her the chocolates that Mum had given me to make up for my jeans.

Hille hesitated. "I should really eat less, but ..." And she'd already unwrapped a chocolate and put it in her mouth.

The next class had begun. German with Dr. Eichenkamp. Normally half the class fell asleep, but today we almost found it fun. At least those of us did who weren't lovesick like me, or who had problems with their holiday jobs like Hille. We were told to make adverts for our school Open Day.

"Leaflets, posters, anything you like," Eichenkamp had said. "The main thing is that you manage to interest as many people as possible in our school, or to get them excited about it. It doesn't matter what method you use to do it."

However, he had then rejected Dirk's suggestion of using a *Playboy* cover picture. Eichenkamp asked Alex to come to the board. He was to write down the class's suggestions. But, of course, nobody had any ideas. Hardly surprising after the stressful Physics test. Alex juggled the chalk and grinned as Oleg started **fooling around** in the back row.

When Jenny got out her pocket mirror and gave herself a loving smile, Eichenkamp had a **nervous breakdown**. "This isn't getting us anywhere," he grumbled, and sent Alex back to his seat.

---

to fool around – herumalbern;
nervous breakdown – Nervenzusammenbruch

Still twenty minutes to go, Hille signalled to me. She pushed a little note over to me. She didn't dare to whisper. Eichenkamp could sometimes turn pretty **nasty**, and at the moment there was already steam coming out of his ears.

Have you got any more chocolates? the note said.

I shook my head.

"Julia!" Our German teacher's voice was a few decibels too loud. I almost jumped out of my skin.

"You've not understood it, have you?"

"Erm, yes, well, of course!" I said. Naturally I didn't have the faintest idea what he was talking about.

"Well, then, explain the **roundabout technique** to everyone once more," Dr. Eichenkamp asked me. "You're very welcome to use an example to do so. But not too **outlandish**, is that clear?"

The roundabout technique? Not too outlandish? What did that have to do with our German class or the Open Day? Maybe the cars were going to be diverted so that the school's only car park wasn't completely blocked? I looked pleadingly in Hille's direction, but she had to pass on that one, too.

"Well, the roundabout technique is ..." I began.

Sometimes that works with Eichenkamp. He absolutely loves hearing himself talk, and I've often found that I've started a sentence only for him to interrupt me right in the middle of what I'm say-

---

nasty – gemein; roundabout technique – Technik des Umwegs; outlandish – abwegig

ing. Then he'd praise me afterwards for apparently having said it so well. I had **to stake my cards on** this.

But it didn't **wash with** Eichenkamp today. He made no move to interrupt me. Instead, he stared at the register which was lying open in front of him, and he scrutinized the long list of absent pupils.

"Have we got an outbreak of the **plague** among you lot?" he asked Benedict in the front row. Then he turned back to me. "Julia, have you got a little bit further, or are you still in the warming-up phase?"

I just shook my head.

"So that you can see how lucky you are, I'll explain it to you all once again," he said, closing the register decisively. "This time it's especially for our dear Julia and also for Alex. I'm sure he didn't get it either, am I right?"

Maybe it was because he mentioned both our names in the same sentence, but at any rate, I suddenly started to pay attention.

"In advertising you can, of course, **blurt out** your message," Dr. Eichenkamp lectured us, walking through the rows as he did so. "In other words, you can tell people in your first sentence what it's all about. For example: buy washing powder X because X washes the whitest ..." He raised his voice.

---

to stake my cards on – auf diese Karte setzen;
to not wash with – nicht ziehen; plague – Pest;
to blurt sth out – mit etw. herausplatzen

He took Jenny's pocket mirror out of her hands. "**Confiscated**! You can have it back on the last day of school." Ignoring her angry protests, he carried on. "... but that's boring. Terribly boring. It makes much more sense to create tension. The person who's receiving the news can easily be left in the dark for a while about what I actually want. For example, if I'm advertising a washing powder, I'll tell a story that has initially nothing to do with it. Only at the end do I then **reveal** which product it's actually about. Is that clear? That's the roundabout technique. Have you all got it now?"

Nobody spoke.

Eichenkamp nodded. "Your homework: think up a good start to the adverts for our school. Try using the roundabout technique. And write it down, just to make sure that we've fully understood one another!" he added after the bell had already gone.

At home I finally had some peace and quiet that day because Mum had taken Timmi to the doctor's. He'd been constantly scratching his head for days, and we weren't sure whether he might not have headlice after all.

I stuffed my meal in the microwave, switched the TV on, and ignored all the annoying demands that Mum had stuck to the kitchen door on yellow sticky notes.

---

to confiscate – konfiszieren;
to reveal – enthüllen

*Unload the **dishwasher**, please!*
Take the rubbish out!

As I took a carton of chocolate mousse out of the **fridge**, I remembered my stained jeans and ran down to the cellar to get them out of the washing machine. No chance: the washing machine had completely failed. The cocoa marks seemed, in fact, to have multiplied – while, by contrast, the jeans had **shrunk** a fair bit. At first I wanted to just throw them away, but when I remembered how expensive they were, I decided to **proceed** systematically. First of all I had to get the stains out; they'd stretch on their own if I wore them often enough. Or that's what I'd always found with jeans in the past.

I fetched some stain remover and a nail-brush and installed myself at the bathroom basin. Then I **scrubbed** with all my **might** at the trousers. The television **blared** away downstairs – adverts – and I was cross that I'd not turned the volume down. Then I remembered the German lesson and the homework, and the more I worked away at the cocoa marks with soap and the nail-brush, the more a thought took shape in the back of my mind.

Of course, *that* was the right technique! The roundabout technique! I'd simply alter it some-

---

dishwasher – Spülmaschine;
fridge – Kühlschrank; to shrink – schrumpfen, eingehen;
to proceed – vorgehen; to scrub – schrubben;
might – Kraft; to blare – dröhnen

what. It was brilliant! Why hadn't I thought of it much earlier? It was in fact staring me in the face. That was the only way I'd manage to go up to Alex all relaxed and say: Alex, I really like you. Shall we go out sometime?

I was so excited about my idea that the remaining marks on my jeans ceased to bother me. Instead, I got straight on the phone after I'd eaten. My idea was so fantastic that Hille could use it for her job-hunt, too, no problem.

My friend sounded quite sleepy when she finally answered the phone on about the thirteenth ring.

"I want to be fit for the interview this afternoon," she explained, yawning. "Fitness is everything nowadays, or so my father says at any rate. Have you already done the homework? If you have, you could quickly dictate a couple of things to me. There's no way now that I'll get round to it today."

"Unfortunately, I couldn't waste my time on trivial **matters** like homework," I giggled.

"Oh, right," said Hille. "Is that why you're in such a good mood?"

"So you've finally got it! Know what? For the first time in my life, I have the feeling that I've actually learnt something at school. Not something stupid like how to calculate **dioptric** values or that sort of thing. You forget that right after the test, at

---

matter – Angelegenheit; dioptric – Dioptrien

the very latest. No: I've learnt something that you can actually use."

"Oh, right," Hille said again, yawning rather loudly. "Could it be that I happen to have missed something? Or are you imagining the whole thing? Whatever, I'm sure you'll **let on** what it is, won't you?" She didn't sound very excited. It was clear to me that I wouldn't be able to **convince** her of my idea over the telephone.

"Hille, you absolutely have to come round. You'll be amazed," I said **beseechingly**. "You can pull out of your interview this afternoon. What I've discovered will solve all your problems. Believe me."

She just laughed. "So, have you got me a job?"

"I didn't say that, but I know how you can solve the problem. And I now know, too, how I can arrange things so that I dare to approach Alex."

That was my **trump** card. Hille stopped short. "And what's that got to do with the other thing?"

"I'll tell you if you come round. Everyone's out, so we'll be totally undisturbed. By the way, I've still got two cartons of chocolate mousse in the fridge."

Maybe it was the reference to chocolate mousse that motivated Hille, but ten minutes later she was standing outside my house.

"So, spit it out," she said, spooning up the mousse that was actually meant for Timmi. "But

---

to let on – verraten; to convince – überzeugen; beseechingly – flehend; trump – Trumpf

get a move on; I've got my appointment in an hour."

In order to keep Hille sweet I fetched the second chocolate mousse from the fridge and put it on the table in front of her.

"Thanks for the mousse. My mother's put me on a diet," she moaned. "So go on, let's hear it."

"You presumably heard how Eichenkamp explained all the details of the roundabout technique in German this morning," I said.

Hille looked at me uncomprehendingly. "Sorry, I wasn't listening at all. I spent the whole time wondering what mark I needed in the Physics test to **scrape through**. Unfortunately, I've got no idea whether I did the third exercise or not. Everything on the test paper was so confusing, you know. All the other teachers use computers, just ..."

"That's not important now," I interrupted her. "You can complain about it tomorrow!"

"Great!" Hille sounded pretty annoyed. "First of all you wake me up and tell me to come and see you as if something amazing had happened. And then you couldn't **give a toss about** my Physics test. There's a lot resting on it for me, I can tell you." She bent forwards towards me. "If you don't tell me your fantastic plan within the next five minutes, then I'm off. I've still got stuff to do. An interview, for instance."

---

to scrape through – einigermaßen durchkommen;
to not give a toss about sth – sich nicht die Bohne für etw. interessieren

I shoved the second carton of mousse right under her nose.

"Five minutes," she repeated, tearing off the lid.

"Okay! I hope you get it that quickly."

Hille just nodded. If she was offended, she did not show it.

"It's quite simple. My problem with Alex is that he's so important to me. I could never say to him: I really like you, or anything like that. I'd start stuttering or I'd go red and wouldn't know where to look and stuff. D'you see what I mean?"

Hille scraped the last bit of mousse out of the carton and nodded. "Got it. Carry on."

I stood up. I thought my idea was so brilliant that I couldn't sit still. "I just have to find a roundabout way."

"A roundabout way?" Hille suppressed a grin. "You mean you're going to attack him from the side, or what?"

"Come on, Hille, **use your brain**! The roundabout way **consists of** me practising elsewhere. I'll go up and **chat** to some boy, then I'll arrange to meet him. That won't be so difficult because I won't be in love with him. When I've practised a couple of times, a hundred percent certain I won't find it difficult to approach Alex any more."

"So you're still in love with him," added Hille. She didn't seem to be that convinced by my plan.

"Obviously," I had to admit, "but then I'll have

---

use your brain – denk nach;
to consist of – bestehen aus; to chat – quatschen

had a bit of practice. I imagine it's a bit like ice skating or in-line skating. The first couple of times I found it terribly stressful, but at some point it seemed quite normal to rollerblade into town or to skate figures. And it'll be exactly the same with Alex, I swear."

"Maybe. And what about my holiday job? You said this funny technique would finally help me to get a job."

I laughed. "Course it will, it's quite easy. You have to do exactly the same as me. Simply apply for a job that you don't want under any circumstances. Then go to the interview and get some experience. When you then apply for a job that you're actually interested in, you'll be completely relaxed. Simply because you know what's what because …" I thought for a moment about how I could explain it to Hille, "… well, because it's like an everyday event for you."

I looked at Hille **inquiringly**. If she was **impressed**, she certainly wasn't showing it in the least.

"Oh, well, I'll think about it," she said simply. "Keep your fingers crossed for me. I've got to be at the industrial estate in twenty minutes. They're looking for someone to **stack** shelves. Maybe **it'll work out** this time. To be honest, I'd prefer not to use roundabouts."

---

inquiringly – fragend;
impressed – beeindruckt; to stack – auffüllen;
it'll work out – es wird sich ergeben

Half an hour later, Mum and Timmi returned. The lice had been a false alarm, but my brother was still scratching his head.

"Just stop it," grumbled Mum, "otherwise everyone'll think we really are **infested**."

She gave me a **hostile** look. "You've still not emptied the dishwasher, and the rubbish still hasn't gone out. Have you at least done your homework?"

I mumbled something that could be interpreted any which way. Then I **made haste** to escape from the kitchen.

"And where are the two cartons of chocolate mousse that were in the fridge this morning?" she called after me.

I went to my room and stared out of the window. I should, in fact, have been doing my homework, but I decided to allow myself a couple of minutes of peace in which to think. Why hadn't Hille reacted enthusiastically to my plan? Maybe it wasn't actually as great as I'd initially thought. And, what's more, it was still **in the lap of the gods** as to whether it really would help me to get Alex. Even if I dared to ask him out for an ice cream, for example ... then that wouldn't mean anything. But all the same, it would be a first step. And if I make contact with him, then he might notice that I'm much nicer than he thinks.

---

to be infested – Ungeziefer haben;
hostile – unfreundlich; to make haste – sich beeilen;
to be in the lap of the gods – in den Sternen stehen

If, if, if ... I thought of my great-grandmother Clara who'd always said in her high, **doddery** voice, "My dear child, if there were no such word as 'if', then everyone would be a millionaire." And then she had smiled in a funny way. Whatever, I'd carry out my plan.

On a piece of **rough paper** I firstly wrote down the individual steps in no particular order. I'd organize them into sequence later on. Kissing, at any rate, was the last thing; that much was for sure. I simply wrote down everything that I knew from romantic films: *Flirting, looking deep into his eyes, telling him that I like him, inviting him for an ice cream, giving him my hand when we meet, and then holding his hand for ages, stumbling and holding onto him ...* **Satisfied**, I **surveyed** my list. Once I'd tried it all out with another boy, then nothing more could really go wrong with Alex.

"Telephone!" cried Mum from downstairs. "I'm going shopping now. Are you somehow expecting me to bring the telephone up to you?"

It was Eileen. I knew immediately that she wanted something.

"So? What are you up to?"

I had to grin. I could hardly say I was just writing a list of everything I was going to do in order to get my hands on Alex.

"Oh, nothing special," I murmured.

---

doddery – zittrig;
rough paper – Schmierblatt;
satisfied – zufrieden; to survey – betrachten

She cleared her throat. "Um, that stuff about the F in History, I thought that was really mean of Napoleon." She went silent. I didn't say anything either. Of course, Eileen wasn't ringing me to **commiserate** with me about my lousy mark.

"I just happened to have heard when Napoleon was talking about the homework ... you know ... and that people can improve and stuff ..." She had finally **lost her thread**, though I had no intention of helping her.

"Yes?" I asked.

"Um, so I wanted to ask you ... you said something about an older brother. I always thought you just had a little brother."

Until recently I hadn't known anything about an older brother either, but I couldn't turn back now. I mumbled something incomprehensible and let Eileen carry on stammering.

"If he was at our school, he had the same teachers as us, didn't he? They must all have been at our school for a hundred years." She found the joke wildly funny. She giggled for at least a minute before she got to the point. "Right. Listen. I reckon most teachers set the same tests every year, don't you think? Couldn't you have a look around and see if you could find your brother's old tests?"

"I'll have a look," I said **graciously**. "But there's not much chance. I think my brother threw most stuff away and ..."

---

to commiserate – Mitleid haben; to lose your thread – den roten Faden verlieren; graciously – gnädig

Eileen interrupted me. "French tests would be particularly brilliant. Julia, you're a treasure for looking. By the way, you're coming to Jenny's summer party, aren't you? Hasn't she invited you yet? Hey, I'll be having words with her. She's just forgotten, for sure. You have to bring a horror film as your entrance ticket, that's what we've agreed on." She giggled stupidly. "And don't forget to look for the tests, okay, promise?"

"Yes," I said graciously. "I'll have a look."

I unloaded the dishwasher. Typical! I have to do that, and my little brother doesn't even **clear away** the thousands of toys that he **scatters** across the living room! Then the doorbell rang like mad. I pressed the buzzer that opened the door and heard Timmi flinging himself at Hille, howling like a **Red Indian**.

"Can't you teach that monster some manners?" she complained once she had freed herself from the lasso that he'd wound around her feet. Even from three kilometres away you could see that Hille's interview had been a **flop** again.

"I just don't understand," she moaned.

I pressed a **tea-towel** into her hand. "If you help me, we can go upstairs in a minute. You've just got to dry the plates off a bit."

Hille made no protest at all. I reckon she'd have

---

to clear away – aufräumen;
to scatter – verstreuen; Red Indian – Indianer;
flop – Reinfall; tea-towel – Geschirrtuch

swept the floor as well and cleaned the windows without complaining, she was so fed up.

"Thousands of other people find a holiday job without any problems, but I just can't do it," she said, polishing away at Timmi's favourite cup with the two mice on it. "I hardly dare to open my mouth for pure fear of saying the wrong thing."

I cleared the **cutlery** away into the drawer and didn't say anything.

"D'you think it's because I'm not incredibly thin?"

"What's that got to do with you not being able to open your mouth?" I asked, confused.

Hille laughed, but it sounded pretty cheerless. "True. You know, I plan what I'm going to say, and then they ask me some stupid question I haven't been expecting. And then I have a complete black-out. I sit there and look like a **startled rabbit**."

I took Timmi's favourite cup, which she was still polishing away at, out of her hands.

"I'm sorry," she said, "I think I'm a bit of a **wet blanket** at the moment. But you know, I was so sure it'd work out this time. After all, they were only looking for someone to stack shelves. Do you have to be able to talk like a politician to do that?"

She sniffed and cast a brief yet longing look at the bar of chocolate that Mum had hidden from Timmi's greedy fingers behind the cups in the cup-board. I broke off four squares, put them on a side

---

cutlery – Besteck; startled rabbit – verängstigtes Kaninchen; wet blanket – Trauerkloß

plate, and looked at Hille. "I reckon we both need something sweet, don't you?"

"I've thought about it," Hille said after a while.

I had in the meantime fetched the rest of the chocolate. If nothing was left, it was less noticeable, I found.

"Maybe your suggestion isn't at all bad. Perhaps I should apply for something that I don't want to do under any circumstances."

I leaned back, satisfied. "Well, that's what I just said. At the next interview you act just as you normally do. And when they offer you the job, you say, 'Thanks, but I've had a re-think. There's no way I want to work for you!'"

The thought of this pleased Hille. She grinned broadly. "Brilliant! These idiots who scrutinize you as if you were an object in an exhibition – I'd like to show them! They'll have to be really keen to give me the job. But I've got no idea what I should apply for. Holiday jobs don't exactly grow on trees. Eileen said she'd got her eye on something in a computer shop. Of course, she got it. And she's not got the faintest idea about computers and – "

"Hille, I've got to tell you something," I interrupted her. "Just imagine this: she rang to ask if I'd already been invited to Jenny's summer party."

"Oh!" Hille's voice sounded mocking. "So you've gone up in the world?"

I shook my head. If I didn't want Hille to turn hideously **jealous**, I had no choice but to tell my

---

jealous – eifersüchtig

friend everything: about my invented brother, the History homework and so on.

Hille roared with laughter when I'd admitted everything. "Wow, is Eileen stupid or what? She thinks she'll get the tests in return for **wangling** you an invitation to Jenny's party. So, what are you going to do now? Alex is invited, too, after all."

I nodded. "But you can imagine, can't you, that I've got absolutely no desire to go to the summer party if he and Jenny are going around all **lovey-dovey**. My only chance is ..." I took a deep breath. "Alex and me: it has to happen before the summer party!"

Hille stood up. "Tests, Open Day, school party, summer party – and Alex on top of that! You've taken a lot on."

I laughed. "Tests, Open Day, school party, and then finding a job. Do you notice anything, Hille?"

She pulled a face. "Yes, of course. I've got a lot on, too. Unfortunately, I'm not invited to Jenny's magnificent summer party. I hope I'll get over it. Or I'll get myself an older sister who's won the Nobel Prize for Maths, Physics and Chemistry. Then I'll get invited to all the summer parties, too."

"Have you thought of a **victim** yet?" Hille asked on the bus the following morning.

---

to wangle – deichseln; lovey-dovey – verliebt; victim – Opfer

"Victim?"

She gave me a meaningful look. "The roundabout technique," she **warbled** cheerfully. "You know what I mean!"

The grey-haired woman sitting opposite us put her newspaper down and examined us in an **exaggeratedly** inconspicuous manner.

I shook my head. "I've not **got round to** it yet. But I'll have a look round at school. Maybe I'll find someone suitable."

The woman had in the meantime moved both her shopping bags slightly to one side, and was leaning forwards. She examined us and appeared to be thinking.

Hille grinned at me. She whispered, "We'll have to shout. I think the woman's deaf." I grinned back. However, it didn't seem to be necessary to speak any louder because the woman was flicking through her paper with an **offended** expression. Giggling, we got off at the next stop. There we **came across** Kevin on the other side of the road.

"He's the one," snorted Hille, almost stumbling over a school bag that someone had simply dumped outside the schoolyard. "Julia, try Kevin: there's no way anything can go wrong there. I can tell you a thing or two about him."

---

to warble – trällern;
exaggeratedly – übertrieben;
to get round to sth – dazu kommen;
offended – beleidigt;
to come across – zufällig treffen

Kevin?

I turned round. I'd only ever noticed Kevin on account of his completely freaky gear. He wore brightly-coloured checked caps, baggy trousers and several T-shirts of different sizes, all on top of one another. Although he was in my class, I'd never had any kind of proper conversation with him. Maybe it was because he spent the whole time listening to music and was **allegedly** only interested in **water polo**.

"Of course!" Hille was all excited. "Kevin's absolutely no problem. Last year, on project days, I was in his group, and he really is okay. A bit mad maybe, but he doesn't **take offence**, guaranteed. I reckon you could start with him."

"I don't know." Kevin was, in fact, not my type, though on the other hand that made the whole thing hugely easier. Yes, of course. Kevin was precisely the right way in for me.

---

allegedly – angeblich;
water polo – Wasserball; to take offence – beleidigt sein

"I'll just think of a strategy," I said. "I'd find it a bit stupid, just going up and talking to him. Perhaps I should change something about the way I look, what do you reckon?"

Hille scrutinized me. "You're right. You don't really go with him at the moment, the way he goes around looking freaky. Maybe you could just cut up a pair of jeans or a T-shirt – "

"Good one," I interrupted. "I can't get the cocoa stains out of my white jeans. So I'll just cut a bit off." I looked at the clock. "But before that we'll have to hear Napoleon **giving us what for**. We're precisely seven minutes late."

Outside the classroom we met Carlo and Sebastian, so Napoleon's **tirade** was shared between the four of us. However, that didn't necessarily make it any more pleasant. In any case, the nasty little man suddenly remembered that he'd set us a written homework almost a week ago and that he wanted to collect it in.

Hille **cursed** at the side of me. "Why didn't I just quickly copy the stuff from you on the bus?"

Napoleon got to our row pretty quickly. No wonder: there wasn't much for him to collect in. Only Nadja, our *wunderkind,* and Sandra had put anything at all down on paper. The others tried tired excuses which gained them an F in Napoleon's notebook.

"I felt sick in the lesson before last and I spent

---

to give sb what for – jmdn. beschimpfen;
tirade – Donnerwetter; to curse – schimpfen

the whole lesson outside in the fresh air," Hille informed him when he planted himself before her.

"In the lesson before last, aha!" Napoleon adopted his commander's look. He thought for a moment. "Catch up with it! Produce it without having to be asked! Is that clear?"

Hille nodded at least three times.

Then Napoleon turned to me. "Now this is the young lady who was keen to have something in writing, isn't it?"

In a recent TV report it was alleged that the English were supposed to have **poisoned** Napoleon. If the real Napoleon was anything like ours, I could understand it only too well.

I nodded.

"And?"

For a moment I had a terrible thought that I'd **inadvertently** left the pages on my desk or on the bus. But then I found in my book the two densely packed pages that would be sure to drive Napoleon out of his mind. It was an A-star at the very least.

"So you've finally made an effort," he **growled**, **heedlessly** taking my homework. "So far as length's concerned, at any rate. Of course, it remains to be seen whether it's any good."

He carried on through the rows demanding homework. Normally I couldn't have cared less how Kevin reacted, but now the situation had changed. Out of the corner of my eye I watched

---

to poison – vergiften; inadvertently – aus Versehen; to growl – knurren; heedlessly – achtlos

how he tipped the contents of his school bag onto the desk – much to Napoleon's **outrage** – and rummaged around in them.

"The homework has to be here somewhere," he kept protesting, even when our History teacher had moved three rows further on. Oleg, of course, hadn't got his homework, but he avoided a bad mark because he could prove – as he said twice – that he was ill during the lesson.

And then Napoleon was standing in front of Alex again. I held my breath. For a moment I thought of calling out loud, "Herr Dieringer, Alex and I did the homework together. You have to give us the same mark for it!" But then, of course, I did not dare yet again. They'd all have stared for certain, especially Eileen and Jennifer, and possibly Alex, too, and he'd have been surprised, and ...

"Pull yourself together!" whispered Hille next to me as Napoleon produced his notebook and entered an F into it. "You'll still get your Alex."

The opportunity to talk to Kevin arose earlier than I'd expected. There was quite a lot to get ready for the Open Day, and everyone was looking for volunteers who were prepared to do something or other. Our class was to take care of the school newspaper and write articles.

"About school, about yourselves, your hobbies, doesn't matter what it's about," said Phillip, our Head Boy. "Something'll occur to you, won't it?

---

outrage – Empörung

And if it doesn't, I've brought you a bunch of essay books from last year. Have a look at them and see if you can find anything useful."

Phillip seemed a bit **irritated** when we bombarded him with questions. "Come on, you all know what a newspaper looks like, don't you? So go and make one. Got it? I've got to go." Then he disappeared, leaving a heap of exercise books on the desk.

"He doesn't have to go round **giving himself airs** just because he's in Year Twelve," complained Rita. "I haven't got a clue what we're supposed to do with all this stuff here."

Eileen and Jenny agreed with her and said that they'd bake a cake after all, and that would be enough work for them. And, anyway, there was to be a salad bar, and someone would have to look after that when all was said and done.

"Okay then, I'll do the stuff with the material for the newspaper," someone said.

Hille prodded me. "Go on!" she hissed. Then she cried loudly, "Hey, Kevin! Julia and I'll do it, too, if that's alright with you."

Kevin shook his head. "Fine by me. Best thing is for us to form a study group. But I want it to go on record that I've done my bit then. So no cake selling or salad bar or anything."

Suddenly other people became interested in the school newspaper. Rita and Diana wanted to form a second study group and suggested organizing

---

irritated – genervt; to give oneself airs – sich aufspielen

the adverts. And Dennis and Matthias offered to write an article.

"I might help you," I heard Alex saying to Rita and Diana. "It's just that I'm not sure at the moment what else I've got on. But let me know when you're meeting, and it might fit in with my plans."

I was really fed up. With Kevin, Hille and with Eichenkamp, who'd given me the stupid idea of the 'roundabout technique' in the first place. That would have been *the* chance. I could have volunteered for the same study group and perhaps ... But now I'd started this whole thing off and I couldn't go back. Maybe it was better that way!

When I looked back at Alex, he smiled at me – and what did I do? Instead of smiling back, I **went beetroot**. No, it was definitely better to practise the flirting stuff a bit before I kept making a fool of myself in front of Alex.

After the last lesson Hille and I agreed with Kevin that we'd meet the following day straight after school at my house to look through the essays and identify suitable articles.

"Hey, listen," Hille informed me on the way home. "Kevin's totally chaotic and the thing he hates most is **bourgeois** people. He told me so when we were in afternoon detention together last year. At any rate, I can't imagine he's changed much. You'll have to **take that into account**."

But, of course, she had no idea either about *how*

---

to go beetroot – eine rote Birne bekommen;
bourgeois – spießig; to take into account – berücksichtigen

I was supposed to take that into account. I sat in my room that afternoon and thought. I really didn't want to snip my white jeans to pieces for Kevin. After all, I could always dye them black.

I fetched Mum's big mirror and stared at myself. Normal, I just looked normal. Long hair, no earrings, no piercings, nothing at all. Quite tall and **slim**, just dead boring. Kevin and I **went together like chalk and cheese**. But I wasn't desperately keen to change my appearance either. After all, Kevin was just the object of an experiment.

I took the mirror back and as I returned to my room, I had a sudden, blinding realization. Of course: I'd change my bedroom! I'd certainly not find it difficult to turn it into a chaotic hole that would satisfy even Kevin's **requirements**. First off I'd have to be parted from the five teddy bears on my bed for a while. I apologized to them all personally as I packed them into a box and shoved it under the bed. Then I pulled some clothes from the wardrobe, spread them around the room, fetched some old magazines from the garage and piled them up on my desk and next to the bed. I scattered my CD collection across the floor along with some books from the shelf. Satisfied, I surveyed my **handiwork**. My room looked as if it hadn't been tidied for months. Even Kevin couldn't possibly have more chaos than this at home.

---

slim – schlank; to go together like chalk and cheese – wie Tag und Nacht sein; requirement – Anspruch; handiwork – Handarbeit

Over breakfast the following morning I informed Mum that Hille and a boy from my class were coming round that afternoon. Of course, she wanted to know more details, but I just said that we had to prepare something for our school newspaper.

"Then you're in luck!" she said. "Timmi won't be at home this afternoon. He's been invited to the house of a friend from kindergarten." She looked at the clock. "Don't tell me Timmi's still asleep. We've got to go in quarter of an hour. Could you just **nip up** and wake him?"

I pulled a face. "**I'm in a bit of a rush**. I was late not long ago and got into quite a lot of trouble with Napoleon." A bit of exaggeration couldn't **do** any **harm**. But I really *didn't* have any time. Because I'd had a marvellous idea. I fetched my old ice skates from the cellar (there's no way anyone could see that they didn't fit me any more), and put them next to my bed.

Now the chaos was perfect. Kevin would feel really at home, and I could practise my flirting.

I was just about to leave the house when Mum called after me, "I'll be back half an hour later than usual at lunchtime. I'll hurry, of course, but … do you want me to make lunch for three if you're bringing Hille and someone else back with you?"

I shook my head, horrified. That was all I needed: some bourgeois lunch in the microwave. Kevin would have a fit on the spot.

---

to nip up – hochflitzen;
to be in a rush – es eilig haben; to do harm – schaden

"No need," I said. "Hille's on a diet, and I really don't have to go eating in front of her."

"And the classmate you want to bring home with you? He'**s bound to be hungry**, surely."

"Kevin's allergic to food," I said. "You surely don't want to poison him."

Mum laughed, but she seemed thoughtful as she did so. "No, of course not. Kevin – isn't that the blond boy who always wears those funny caps?"

"It could well be. See you, I've got to **rush**." I ran off before Mum could ask me any more **nosey** questions.

Hille, we'd agreed, would get the bus part of the way with us after school. Then she'd suddenly remember that she had an interview that very afternoon.

"I'll leave you then," she said as we waited for Kevin after the sixth period. "I'll give you a ring at around half three to hear how it's going. And remember, nothing's at stake."

I nodded. "Too right: nothing's at stake." In truth, I was already feeling quite uncomfortable. I had seen Alex running to the bus stop. He'd suddenly stopped and had stared at me for a moment. Did he want to say something to me? Or had I just imagined it?

Carlo and Robert strolled across the schoolyard.

---

to be bound to be hungry – sicher hungrig sein;
to rush – sich beeilen; nosey – neugierig

"Hey, d'you know where Kevin's got to?" Hille called to them.

"He's running round the whole school looking for his cap," laughed Robert. "I reckon he didn't even have the cap on this morning. He's just totally chaotic, that idiot. How on earth can someone make such a fuss?" Carlo stood by silently.

I was gradually starting to find the whole thing not in the slightest bit funny. The next bus left in five minutes and if we didn't get a move on, we'd have to wait half an hour for the one after that.

"Well, at last!" Hille also sounded pretty fed up once Kevin – with his cap – was finally standing in front of us. We sprinted to the bus stop, just managed to catch our bus, and fought our way through a horde of primary school kids who, with their huge **satchels**, naturally had a great advantage over us to get to some seats.

"So we'll go through all the essays and see whether they might possibly fit into the school newspaper," I said, just to say something. "Should we correct all the mistakes, or shall we just copy them?" I looked directly at Kevin as I spoke, which wasn't easy as he was wearing mirrored sunglasses and I could only make a **rough guess** at where his eyes were.

"Apparently they're going to be typed up by the school secretary," he said after a while. "I actually wanted to write a poem for the school newspaper, but then I forgot somehow and now ..."

---

satchel – Ranzen; rough – grob; guess – Schätzung

"Oh God!" Hille had jumped up. "I'd almost forgotten something, too. I've got an interview this afternoon. Damn!" She looked at me inquiringly. "Hey, could you possibly get started without me? This interview is really important to me."

Hille was a born actress. For a moment I actually believed her.

"Of course," Kevin said for me, "we'll just get started. But don't think we're going to do all the work on our own."

"Of course not!" Hille laughed. "Please do leave something for me to do. I'll give you a ring soon, once the interview's over, and I'll come round. Okay?"

"Good luck," I called after her as she got off at the next stop. Then Kevin and I were sitting opposite one another in silence. It wasn't bad because the primary school kids all around us were making **tons of** noise.

"So this is where you live," he stated **astutely** as I opened the front door. It was the first thing he'd said since Hille had got off.

I nodded. At that moment I didn't feel like flirting. I would, in fact, have preferred to have some peace and quiet, but I'd come up with this whole business, and at the end of the day I was just doing it all for Alex.

Alex has grey-blue eyes, not blue ones as I'd thought until recently. Grey-blue like the sea on

---

tons of – jede Menge; astutely – scharfsinnig

an October afternoon when it turns cooler and the seagulls cry and everything's all lonely.

"Hey, Julia, what's up?" Kevin poked me in the side. "You're sitting there looking all weird. Shouldn't we finally get started? Have you got any Coke or anything?"

I nodded. "Yes, you just go on upstairs! Second door on the right. But watch out you don't fall over anything," I added. "I have tidied up, but I just can't get rid of the chaos."

I thought this was a brilliant remark. With a bit of imagination Kevin would be able to picture what it must have looked like before I tidied up.

"Doesn't bother me, I'm used to it," he said and went upstairs whilst I looked in the fridge for two cans of Coke.

"Julia?"

I span round. Mum was home. This early?

"Just ask Kevin if he can eat fish fingers with chips and salad. The salad is for Hille because she –"

"I thought you were going to be back later?" I said, **baffled**. Oh great. My mother was standing in the dining room door and was bound to wreck everything for me. She'd probably eat with us and keep an eye on our table manners. I knew that game!

"Timmi's got some kind of childhood **ailment**," she said, "a **rash** on his face, but the doctor told me on the phone that it probably wasn't **conta-**

---

baffled – verdutzt; ailment – Krankheit; rash – Ausschlag

gious. So he can quite happily eat with us. Maybe Kevin would like to meet your brother, too."

I stared at her, my mouth open. What an idiot I was! Why hadn't I realized earlier? Mum, of course, thought that Kevin was the reason why I was lovesick, and now she was absolutely desperate to meet him and, probably, to show him our family's best side. I wouldn't have been surprised if she had cleaned the whole house for this purpose.

I had a terrible thought.

"So what about the food?" she called after me as I raced up the stairs.

I flung the bedroom door open. It was just as I'd feared: my magnificent chaos had gone, just gone. Instead, my mother had gone to great efforts to tidy my room and to make it look really nice: a floral bedspread, a bunch of roses on the desk and, next to it, a plate of biscuits. Nothing was left of my brilliant plan. My five teddy bears were back in their old place but all the clothes had disappeared back into the wardrobe, and even the broken desk drawer which wouldn't close any more had been repaired. It seemed that the ice skates were the only things that she hadn't had time to clear away: like unnecessary remains of a chaotic past, they were standing next to my rocking chair. The window was half open and the room was filled with the honeyed **scent** of roses.

Kevin was sitting neatly on the chair next to my desk and barely seemed to dare unpack his school-

---

contagious – ansteckend; scent – Duft

bag. He was probably totally **overwhelmed** by the orderliness in my room.

I heard Mum coming up the stairs. It was mega-embarrassing. She'd offer him her hand and say something pleasant. "How nice to meet you at last, Kevin," or something like that. And I'd sink into the ground. And on top of that, how was I supposed to explain to her that Hille wasn't here?

Timmi was yelling in the corridor. This time he'd be my **salvation**. I wrenched the door open – and **recoiled**.

"Boo!" said my brother and twisted his face – which was covered in little red spots – into a **grimace**. "I'm poisonous, and you'll get it, too, and then nobody will in love with you because you're so – "

"You'll have to learn to speak English first," I said nastily. I slammed the door. When I was eighteen, I was moving out, that much was for sure.

Kevin was still sitting as if nailed to the chair.

"Your brother?"

I nodded. I didn't want to say anything more. Everything could only go even worse.

Mum had **carted** Timmi back off to bed. She knocked on my bedroom door. I'd have liked to say, "No, you're disturbing us," but then I didn't dare after all. As my parent, she probably had free **access** to my room until I was eighteen. She was

---

overwhelmed – überwältigt; salvation – Rettung; to recoil – zurückschrecken; grimace – Grimasse; to cart – verfrachten; access – Zutritt

already standing in the middle of the room with this pseudo-astonished expression.

"Ah, you must be Kevin?" she cried, going up to him with her hand outstretched. "How nice to meet you!" That was probably what she called a warm greeting. I had to do something before she could possibly say that I'd talked so much about him and how delighted she was and so on.

"Christine!" I said, my tone deadly serious. "Mum" would have sounded too childish at that moment.

She turned round, astonished.

"Timmi ... the rash ... um, I think it's highly contagious. We read something about it in Biology recently and I'm worried that Kevin ..."

Pull yourself together, don't stammer!, I thought, but I could barely construct a single clear thought. The only thing I knew was this: Kevin had to disappear as quickly as possible.

"Unfortunately, I couldn't get an appointment until this evening," said Mum regretfully, "but on the phone the doctor said it probably wasn't measles and ..."

"Yes, measles!" I nodded vigorously. "Exactly! There's a new type, and it's incredibly contagious. Kevin, you'd better leave at once, I don't want you to catch it."

Kevin just stared at me. "I've had measles at least twice; that doesn't worry me in the slightest."

Mum smiled, **relieved**. "Well then, everything's

---

relieved – erleichtert

hunky-dory. The chips are already in the oven, and I'll have the fish fingers ready in ten minutes. Do you like green salad, Kevin?"

"Of course," he said without **batting an eyelid**. "Of course, I like green salad."

I didn't know who I would have preferred to get lost: my mother, who was winking **conspiratorially** at me after Kevin had assured her that he didn't have any food allergies so far as he knew and that chips and fish fingers were one of his favourite meals. Or Kevin, this supposedly chaotic classmate, who seemed to be really looking forward to a bourgeois lunch.

At any rate, he ran downstairs when my mother called us to eat ten minutes later. And even the sight of my **spotty-faced** brother wasn't enough to put him off devouring vast quantities of food.

Mum looked quite happy, especially when she noticed that Kevin was even using the napkin that she'd put next to his plate. And, what's more, he didn't once speak with his mouth full.

"I'm just going back upstairs," I murmured after lunch. If I'd been hoping to get Kevin away from the table, I'd been hugely mistaken. He was talking to Timmi about the advantages of **stunt kites** and seemed quite happy about it.

"I'm going upstairs now," I repeated loudly, and

---

hunky-dory – toll;
to bat an eyelid – mit der Wimper zu zucken;
conspiratorially – verschwörerisch;
spotty-faced – pickelgesichtig; stunt kite – Lenkdrachen

Kevin said he'd be up in a minute. He'd just clear the table first.

My eyes almost popped out of my head. This was just unbelievable! Chaotic Kevin turns out to be a model boy and **behaves** like a prospective **son-in-law**. My mother, at any rate, had completely melted and was just opening a packet of chocolates. "For pudding," as she said.

I waited in my room until Kevin was finally full. I had absolutely no desire to flirt now. My mother would probably appear in the next half an hour with a kitchen tray because she thought Kevin was so charming. I found it all **nauseating**.

"Are you in a bad mood, or what?" Kevin asked at the door. He flopped down into my rocking chair. "Your mother's a really good cook." He **yawned** half audibly. "Wow, I'm stuffed. Have you by any chance had a look at the stuff?" He gesticulated to his schoolbag and yawned again.

"No, I haven't."

He shrugged his shoulders. "I only asked. In fact, it's almost too late to do any work now, and Hille's not here either ... Shall we **postpone** the whole thing?"

"Yeah, let's postpone it. I don't have to show you out, I'm sure you'll find your own way," I muttered.

He stood up, **clasped** his schoolbag under his

---

to behave – sich verhalten; son-in-law – Schwiegersohn;
nauseating – widerlich; to yawn – gähnen;
to postpone – verschieben; to clasp – klemmen

arm, and yawned again. I was pretty sure that he'd have an afternoon sleep as soon as he got home. I heard Mum's voice in the stairwell. Kevin seemed to be saying goodbye to her. I wanted to cry. Kevin was bourgeois **with knobs on**.

Mum came into my room without knocking. She made out as if she just wanted to give the flowers some fresh water.

"What's that face for?" she wanted to know. "Kevin really is an extremely well **brought up** young man. You can bring him round as often as you like, no problem. Isn't his father a dentist?"

"Dunno," I growled. "But I hardly think he'll come again." Mum had plonked herself down on my bed. When she saw my face, she smiled.

"People often **quarrel** at your age, but they **make it up** again just as quickly. Everything's sure to turn out the way you want it to."

I hope so, I wanted to say, but I bit it back.

"So chin up, it'll be fine," she concluded. "Do you **fancy** a praline?" I shook my head. No thanks, I'd lost my appetite.

There still seemed to be something bothering my mother. At any rate, she **plucked** away at the bunch of flowers on my desk for a remarkably long time. The telephone rang downstairs, but she ignored it. I just wanted to run down, but she shook her head.

---

with knobs on – und wie!; brought up – erzogen;
to quarrel – streiten; to make it up – sich versöhnen;
to fancy – (hier:) wollen; to pluck – pflücken

"Julia, we're not going to be disturbed by the telephone. There's something I want to discuss with you quickly."

She sat herself next to me and took me half in her arms. "Hey, Julia, wasn't Hille going to come, too? You know, perhaps it's not so good if you bring Kevin home when nobody's here. I think he's quite charming, but ..."

"But you were here!"

"Yes, but I wasn't actually supposed to be back until later." She looked at me, at a loss. "Get me right, Julia. You and Kevin are in love with one another and ..."

The telephone rang again.

"I'm not in love with Kevin and Kevin's not in love with me," I said decisively. "If you want to know the truth: Kevin was just supposed to be my **guinea pig**."

I **spared myself** my mother's reaction. I ran down the stairs and was about to answer the phone, but the answering machine had already come on and I heard Hille's voice. "Is everything okay there? Have you already driven him half wild?" she giggled. "I hope I'm not disturbing you. Can you come round at around half four and tell me everything? Bye, see you later."

I looked up the stairs. If Mum had heard that, she'd have a moderate fit. I slipped up to my room, stuffed the biscuits, so lovingly arranged on

---

guinea pig – Versuchskaninchen (eigentlich Meerschweinchen); to spare oneself – sich schenken

the plate next to the flowers, into my mouth, and dreamed of grey-blue eyes and more besides.

Gone to doctor early just to be on the safe side, it said on the note that Mum had stuck to the pinboard. *PS: Keep your fingers crossed that it's not as* ***infectious*** *as you feared!*

I scribbled *Will do. Gone to Hille's!* underneath it before I went out.

I actually wanted to go by bike, but there wasn't much air in my front **tyre** and I simply couldn't find the bicycle pump anywhere in the garage. I should have taken Kevin into the garage, I thought. There was such a hideous mess in there that even he would have been impressed. But that had all happened now. I had to face facts.

I rang Hille's bell at around four, but nobody answered. For a moment I was on the point of being really fed up, but then I wasn't sure whether she'd said four or four thirty, and I decided to give Hille another chance.

I strolled through the streets wondering if I should go to town and buy myself something. I did after all have seven euros left over from my birthday, but I didn't really want to go wandering around town.

Then I spotted Carlo on the other side of the road. Normally I wouldn't have given him a second **glance**, but things looked different now. Maybe I could chat to him until Hille turned up.

---

infectious – ansteckend; tyre – Reifen; glance – Blick

I'd known Carlo since kindergarten. The pair of us had driven at least three kindergarten teachers mad because we had kept climbing the tree outside the kindergarten. This was, of course, strictly forbidden, but that had never bothered Carlo any more than it bothered me. The old **chestnut** tree had long since been **felled**. Someone was supposed to be installing a **bus shelter** there, but somehow it never happened. Sometimes I felt sad when I cycled past the kindergarten and saw the empty space. Did Carlo still remember that tree?

I crossed the road and made directly for him. He **blinked at** me. He'd barely changed since kindergarten. He had, it was true, got taller and older, but his facial expression was still the same: a bit disbelieving, a bit dreamy.

I would never – and I was firmly convinced of this – fall in love with him. What's more, he wasn't as strange as Kevin. Carlo was simply a perfectly normal boy. Precisely the right victim for me, then.

"Helloo," I said, drawing out the word and trying to make my voice sound deeper. Eileen had recently done that when she rang Alex. I thought it had been massively effective.

"Hello," said Carlo, fishing a **cough sweet** from his right trouser pocket. "**Sage** helps, so my grandmother always says."

---

chestnut – Kastanie; to fell – fällen;
bus shelter – Bushaltestelle; to blink at – anblinzeln;
cough sweet – Hustenbonbon; sage – Salbei

I looked at him, baffled. "Sage? Helps against what?"

"**Colds**, what do you think?" He shook his head and put his sweet away. He seemed to be a bit offended. "Your voice sounds **dreadful** at any rate."

I decided **discreetly** to switch back to a normal tone of voice.

"It's really cold weather at the moment." He looked at me **searchingly** and I felt a faint **tickle** in my **throat**.

"I was going to visit Hille, but she's not there," I informed him, standing directly in front of him.

He took a step backwards – for fear of catching something from me, perhaps – and looked at me **uncomprehendingly**.

"And what are you doing here?" I added in a friendly manner.

Carlo took a further step back and tried discreetly to hide behind his back the **bundle** he was carrying in his left hand. "I've got something to do," he said finally as if it had just occurred to him. "But now I've got to go."

"I'll walk a bit of the way with you," I said quickly and decisively. My voice trembled **imperceptibly**, even though I wasn't in the slightest bit interested in Carlo.

---

cold – Erkältung; dreadful – grauenhaft;
discreetly – unauffällig; searchingly – forschend;
tickle – Kribbeln; throat – Hals;
uncomprehendingly – verständnislos;
bundle – Beutel; imperceptibly – unmerklich

What would he think of me just walking along with him? We were, it's true, at kindergarten together. But I couldn't remember having had any kind of private conversations with him in the last few years since he switched from the parallel class into my class.

He was silent. We trotted along the **pavement** together, him right on the **kerb** and me almost touching the fences of the front gardens. Half the class would have fitted into the space between us.

"Do you live around here?" I asked eventually when the silence started to become embarrassing.

"Nah."

I swallowed. I'd have liked to tell Carlo how stupid I thought he was, and that he shouldn't get ideas. That he was just a practice object for me, nothing more than that. But, of course, I didn't say a word. I wanted to carry out my plan come what may.

"Have you already done the homework?" I asked him instead.

He turned his head briefly to one side, nodded, took a **hanky** out, and sneezed. I could have shaken him. Not that I'd expected him to be a friendly conversation partner. That would definitely have been impossible with Carlo, what with that dreamy look. But he could at least have made a bit of an effort. I made one last attempt.

"How did you find Physics?"

---

pavement – Gehweg; kerb – Bordsteinkante;
hanky (handkerchief) – Taschentuch

"Good!" He had stopped.

Should I perhaps say now: Hey, Carlo, I think you're pretty interesting. Do you want to give me your phone number? I'll give you a ring sometime!

Whilst I was still standing there undecided, he gesticulated behind me. I turned round and had to grin.

"Oh, wow!" slipped out of me.

In the front garden of the pink two-storey house at least twenty **garden gnomes** were standing arranged in groups of four. Mum would have had a hissy fit. Garden gnomes and nodding dogs in the rear windows of cars came second only to snakes and mice on her list of horrors.

"Well, bye then," said Carlo. "I've got to go in there." He shifted nervously from one leg to the other.

"I've got to go, too," I said. I didn't want to overdo it right at our first **encounter**. Next day, in the schoolyard, I'd **venture** to take the next step.

Carlo seemed quite happy that I was finally going to disappear. At any rate, he smiled now and actually didn't look so bad at all. He was just about to open the garden gate when one of the windows on the ground floor was **flung open**, and ... I probably didn't look very intelligent at that moment. But nobody on earth could have expected this one!

---

garden gnome – Gartenzwerg; encounter – Treffen; to venture – wagen; to fling open – aufreißen

"Carlo! Great that you're here. Have you got her with you?" cried Alex, beaming. "I'll press the door-opener, okay?"

Alex lived here. Carlo was visiting Alex. And I was there. I could have danced or cried or goodness knows what else for joy. This would be a starting point tomorrow break. I could ask him for example why the garden gnomes were arranged into groups of four.

"Well, bye then," Carlo repeated and tried to open the garden gate. The door-opener buzzed, but the gate didn't budge a millimetre. Just like me. I stood there **as if I'd taken root**.

"I'll come out. Something seems to be sticking there," said Alex through the **intercom**.

Carlo was still shaking the garden gate. "I thought you were going to go," he murmured, turning to me.

I ignored his remark. If Alex opened the garden gate, I'd immediately be in: that was plain to see. I simply had to take this chance. And moreover Carlo was there, and his presence made me feel more **secure**, funnily enough.

Alex came along the narrow gravel path, and I had to shut my eyes for a whole short moment. He was simply incredibly good looking. I could just imagine Eileen and Jenny's faces once I started walking across the schoolyard hand in hand with him.

---

as if I'd taken root – wie angewachsen;
intercom – Sprechanlage; secure – sicher

"Hey, I never thought you'd bring her here so quickly," he said to Carlo, leaning over the fence.

I stopped short. What did he mean by that? There's no way he could have known that I'd happen to cross paths with Carlo. But maybe it was that well-known thing called **fate** that was to bring us together. I thanked my lucky stars that I'd put on a fresh T-shirt and that I'd cleaned my teeth after all those biscuits.

Carlo had turned a light shade of red. He hummed and hawed about how he'd just been in the area anyway and that they'd been lying around in the **attic** for months anyway.

Now at the latest I realized that hearing "her" had been a simple case of wishful thinking. Alex didn't seem to be particularly **overjoyed** by my presence either. To tell the truth, he just said a brief "Hi" to me.

"So," Carlo ended his stammering, "are you going to open up now?" Alex shook his head regretfully. "Something's wrong with the door-opener. And modern technology won't allow you to do anything by hand. But just hand over the bag. I'll give you the money tomorrow."

With a **tortured** smile, Carlo handed him the package over the fence. I had the feeling that he found the whole thing more than embarrassing. He looked away as Alex unpacked excitedly.

---

fate – Schicksal; attic – Dachgeschoss;
overjoyed – überglücklich;
tortured – gequält

"Comics?

Mickey Mouse comics?" Hille looked at me despairingly. "Are you sure?"

I nodded and shifted around on Hille's two-seater sofa. "Do you think that's stupid?"

She span round twice on the chair at her desk. "Don't know. It is a bit funny. Mickey Mouse! That's what primary school kids read, isn't it?"

That's exactly what I'd initially thought, too. Carlo had tried to pull me away from the fence and had murmured that I really should go, but I simply stayed put. Then he had given me a **long-winded** explanation that they were his younger brother's comics and that he was selling them for him, but I wasn't in the slightest bit interested in any of that. The more I thought about it, the less I **minded** that Alex was a fan of Mickey Mouse comics. In fact, it was even quite nice. When most adults think that young people are only interested in horror and action.

---

long-winded – langatmig; to mind – etw. ausmachen

I said that to Hille, too, but she just told me that she didn't care, and wanted to know what had happened next with Carlo. After what had happened to me with Kevin, she said, I **deserved** some success.

I laughed. "Poor Carlo was **in a complete daze**. He was so embarrassed, you just can't imagine! He was probably afraid I'd immediately spread it round our class that he reads Mickey Mouse. In any case, he mentioned at least twice more in passing that he'd got the comics from his brother and that he was selling them to Alex for him. But I don't believe a word of it!"

"So it was no good with Kevin," stated Hille. "It'll presumably be Carlo then, will it?" She examined me thoughtfully.

I shrugged my shoulders. "Carlo? Probably yes. So far, everything's going fantastically. I just went up to talk to him and went to Alex's house with him. Just imagine it! Of course, I didn't have the faintest idea where we'd end up. And then I spent ten more minutes hearing the story of his brother and all the comics. But the **crucial** thing is," I stood up and stretched, "that I know where Alex lives now, and I know that he likes reading Mickey Mouse comics, and – "

"Has garden gnomes outside his house," Hille finished my sentence. "You do know you only have me and nobody else to thank for all of this."

---

to deserve – verdienen;
in a complete daze – schön daneben; crucial – wichtig

"You?"

"Of course!" She laughed. "If I'd been in before, then you'd never have met Carlo. Could you do me a favour, too?"

"What favour?" I said suspiciously.

The week before last Hille had borrowed a CD from me and had immediately lost it. What's more, it wasn't remotely Hille's doing: it was entirely thanks to my plan and my determination that I'd made progress. When I saw my friend's face, I decided to say nothing, but just nodded.

"Could you just go down to my mum in the kitchen and tell her that you've not had any lunch?" She pointed to her stomach. "I feel really sick. My mother reckons she has to turn me into a **beanpole** within the next three weeks. She thinks I'll never get a holiday job and never get an **apprenticeship** otherwise. And it goes without saying that I'll never get a man to share my life with."

She sighed. "The stuff I'm getting at the moment calls itself Low-Cal food. You could also say: quarter portions of everything. Go and get me a couple of cheese sandwiches and some bread and jam, would you? If you're hungry, too, then three with cheese and two with jam."

I waved that idea aside. "I'm still completely stuffed." It was undoubtedly better not to tell her that I'd just **gobbled up** an entire packet of chocolate biscuits. I felt rather sorry for Hille. True, she

---

beanpole – Bohnenstange;
apprenticeship – Ausbildung; to gobble up – verdrücken

wasn't exactly thin, but that was by no means a reason to let her starve.

"Two cheese sandwiches and one jam," I repeated and clicked my heels together. "I'll fetch them, Hille, 'course I will."

Her mother was sitting at the kitchen table, smoking and reading a newspaper. She looked up as I stood in the door. "Are you looking for something?"

Well, it *was* a bit embarrassing for me, but at the end of the day I was doing it for Hille.

"Unfortunately, I didn't get any lunch today," I declared. "My brother was ill, and so my mother didn't have time to cook. And now I feel quite sick with hunger. Could I possibly make myself a cheese sandwich ..."

"But you can't have cheese sandwiches!" Frau Ebler had stood up. "I've still got some tasty pasta bake in the fridge from lunchtime. If you wait two minutes, I'll quickly stick it in the microwave, and ..."

"That's much too much trouble," I interrupted. "Perhaps I could just have a couple of pieces of bread with cheese and one with jam."

Hille's mother shook her head vigorously. "You have to have a hot meal. Or you'll just spend the whole day grazing. That makes you fat."

I should have pointed out that I was absolutely not fat and that I'd probably never become fat either, but she had already stuffed the pasta bake in the microwave and had fetched a plate and cutlery.

I felt very sick, but definitely not with hunger. For one thing, I'd seen that it was a spinach pasta bake, something that didn't necessarily belong on my list of favourite meals. For another, I was absolutely not hungry; in fact, I felt as if I wouldn't be able to eat for the next three days. And thirdly – and this was the most important thing – my friend Hille was sitting two doors away, **longing for** me to bring sandwiches and save her from starvation.

I made one last attempt and suggested to Frau Ebler that I could go and eat in Hille's room. "I don't want to disturb you here in the kitchen," I said.

She, however, just laughed and said that **on the contrary**, I wouldn't disturb her in the least, and that in any case it was important for Hille not to see food until supper time.

"Unfortunately, her grandmother fed her completely wrongly," she sighed, heaping a gigantic portion of pasta bake onto the plate. "At some point, Hille will suffer because of her figure. That's why she has to start losing a few kilos now."

She said she hoped I enjoyed my meal, and sat opposite me with her newspaper. I stared into the spinach bake and **hovered** over it with my fork like an **eagle**.

Frau Ebler looked up briefly. "Don't you like it?"

---

to long for sth – auf etw. sehnsüchtig warten;
on the contrary – im Gegenteil;
to hover – schweben;
eagle – Adler

she asked, concerned. "You're very welcome to add some more salt."

"It's just too hot," I explained, blowing on it a bit. If only Hille would come now! Together, we might be able to think of something.

I took a **tiny** mouthful and wondered whether Frau Ebler might possibly buy a severe spinach allergy on my part. But I'd have needed to mention it earlier.

The pasta bake tasted **revoltingly** of spinach. I was almost sick. I'd just decided to push my plate aside and tell Hille's mother that I wasn't that hungry after all, when the telephone rang.

If I was in luck, Frau Ebler would get up and go into the hall. Then I could …

But of course, I wasn't in luck.

"Telephone," I said after the fifth ring.

Frau Ebler just smiled mildly. "It's mostly for Hille in any case. She can get it herself. A bit of activity won't hurt her. Have you got enough pasta bake? What about a bit of pudding? **Home made**!" She put a bowl of red fruit pudding with vanilla sauce on the table. "You like this, don't you?"

I just shook my head and stared at the food on my fork. Would I terminally **offend** Hille's mother if I told her that I couldn't eat the pasta bake with the best will in the world?

---

tiny – winzig;
revoltingly – grauenhaft;
home made – selbst gemacht;
to offend – beleidigen

"Telephone for you!" Hille had **burst** into the kitchen, holding the cordless phone out to her mother. "Why exactly do *I* always have to answer it?"

She stared at the table and spotted the spinach bake and the red fruit pudding. "Julia, I thought you were ..." she began – but then she broke off mid-sentence, turned round and slammed the door behind her.

"No, Mum, Hille isn't coming to eat with you tomorrow," I heard Frau Ebler saying exaggeratedly loudly into the telephone. "I'm taking care of her meals, and it's going **splendidly**. No, she certainly won't starve, you can rely on me."

I pushed the plate aside, murmured that I was already completely stuffed and fled from the kitchen. By now I **couldn't care less** what Frau Ebler thought of me.

It was exactly as I'd feared. Hille was lying on her bed in her room, staring straight ahead.

"It's incredibly reassuring to have a friend who helps you," she said quietly. "You'd better disappear before I turn really angry."

"Hille, this is the honest truth, there wasn't any other way! Your mother forced me to sit at the table and eat. I was almost sick and ..."

"I feel sick, too! Because I think you're all so stupid!" cried Hille. "Gran spent years fattening me

---

to burst – (hier) stürmen;
splendidly – super;
to not care less – etw. ist jmdm. egal

up, and my mother wasn't in the slightest bit interested in me. And then she suddenly remembers that I exist, too, and she declares that this child is much too fat. So let's simply put Hille on a diet. For God's sake! Couldn't she have thought of all this earlier? She knows what Gran's cooking is like." Hille **sniffed** vigorously. "It's probably embarrassing for you, too, having a fat friend."

I shook my head. "That's total **rubbish**. Please believe me, I didn't want the spinach bake at all, but your mother ..."

Hille appeared not to be listening to me. She had stood up and was looking me up and down. "I may not be thin, but I am at least pretty," she said slowly. "Perhaps you should re-think your haircut. Long hair doesn't really suit you, you know. It just hangs there. I hardly think that Alex is into that."

Stupid Hille! For her I let myself be half poisoned by a completely **inedible** spinach bake, risked trouble with her mother for dashing out of the kitchen without eating it up, and then had such **pleasantries** thrown in my face. I'm not taking that, no thank you!

"I do think that Alex is into it," I said simply. I'd have liked to add, "more than he's into your kilos," but that would have been too mean.

I snapped my rucksack shut and didn't **deign to**

---

to sniff – schniefen; rubbish – Quatsch;
inedible – ungenießbar; pleasantry – Nettigkeit;
to deign to do sth – sich herablassen etw. zu tun

look at Hille again. She'd see how she'd manage without me.

Angry, I went home. The whole day had been one long **let-down**. Ideally, I'd have gone home via Alex's house and sobbed something out to him and have had him comfort me. But then I remembered that the garden gate outside his house didn't open. And when I imagined sobbing outside the garden fence with Alex standing on the other side, I almost had to laugh again already.

"False alarm," Mum greeted me when I got home, pleased. "The doctor says it's just a harmless rash. So we can go walking at the weekend. Are you looking forward to it?"

"Of course," I said in a **sepulchral** voice. "I can't imagine anything nicer than walking through the Black Forest with my parents and my bright-red-spotty brother."

I wanted to cry. Walking with my family: that was pretty much the second-worst thing that could happen to me after Hille's mother's spinach bake.

"Kevin's very welcome to come if he likes," said Mum. It sounded so **off-the-cuff**, but I noticed that she was looking at me very closely. She probably thought I'd be pleased. I urgently had to clarify matters. "Kevin doesn't go walking, and in any case I couldn't give a toss about him. He just hap-

---

let-down – Reinfall;
sepulchral – düster; off-the-cuff – spontan

pens to be in my class, and that's that. Could you stop going on at me about the subject!"

I could hear Dad **clattering** around in the hall, but he didn't dare come into the living room. Of course, he'd heard how angry I was.

"And what's more," I added, "everyone thinks that Timmi's got something terribly wrong with him. The way he looks, with those hideous red spots all over his face. And you want to go walking with him?"

That was clear to my mother, too. She was just suggesting that Dad and I go on our own when he came into the living room and interrupted.

"Hey, if Julia doesn't want to go walking, then nobody should force her," he said, thereby ending the discussion. "Anyway, we've got visitors coming on Sunday."

"**Well, there you go**," I said and disappeared into my room. Why didn't we start with that, I added to myself. Why do mothers always have to kick up a huge fuss first?

And Hille was even worse! She had just acted as if I'd **betrayed** her! She could **stuff** her rotten pasta bake! In fact, anyone who ate it would be bound to lose weight, as there's no way anyone could get more than one mouthful down. And the things Hille had said about my hair!

---

to clatter – rumoren;
Well, there you go – Na, also;
to betray – betrügen;
to stuff sth – sich etw. an den Hut stecken

Just to be on the safe side, I fetched the mirror again. Perhaps she was right after all. I used my nail scissors to snip away a bit at my hair, but I wasn't really satisfied with that either.

For a moment I wanted to ring my friend and ask her what she thought I could do about my hair. But then I remembered that we'd **fallen out**, and I decided not to get in touch with her. She could phone me! After all, she'd started it!

But Hille didn't get in touch. Not on Friday evening, and not on Saturday. On Sunday afternoon, when my parents had the Dobenhubers round, I decided simply to act as if nothing had happened and to give her a ring. I needed someone to talk to, about Alex for one thing. And our argument hadn't been that bad.

I stood undecided by the telephone for a couple of minutes, then I rang. But Hille's mother said Hille wasn't there. Hille had just left the house a couple of minutes ago, she said. She was going to meet some kids from school, probably at the swimming baths, because Hille had packed her swimsuit. Didn't I know anything about it? I said, of course, I did and that I'd just forgotten, and replaced the receiver.

My best friend Hille! Barely had she fallen out with me, and she already had new friends. And me? I wondered whether to call Jenny or Rita, then decided against it after all. I would just take myself off to my room, lock the door, and write

---

to fall out – sich zerstreiten

my diary. My last dream had clearly shown me how much I loved Alex. We'd looked at Mickey Mouse comics together and had kissed over and over again.

Suddenly I had a brilliant idea. Timmi also had a couple of comics. I'd wangle them out of him and give them to Alex. Beautifully wrapped, naturally, and maybe **equipped with** a little letter! I instantly felt better. So far as I was concerned, Hille could go to the swimming baths with whoever she liked – I had more important things to do! I ran down the stairs – and straight into Herr Dobenhuber's arms.

"Well, Julia," he **marvelled** yet again. "Haven't you grown? How's school? Are you looking forward to the holidays?" He laughed loudly, shaking my hand.

I just nodded and hoped that his wife wouldn't ask me the same stupid questions.

But Frau Dobenhuber just smiled at me and said I really was very grown up and she was quite sure she could **entrust** the children to me for the next two hours. I swallowed.

"The playground would be the best place," Frau Dobenhuber suggested cheerfully. "You must go there all the time with Timmi. You just have to take care that Deborah and Vanessa don't go too mad on the swings. They always get sick so quickly."

---

equipped with – versehen mit;
to marvel – staunen;
to entrust – anvertrauen

Deborah, Vanessa and Kai-Willem, the youngest, with Timmi to cap it all! A Sunday afternoon at the playground with these brats – that wasn't actually how I'd imagined spending my day.

So, with the four children in tow, I went to the playground, hoping that I wouldn't bump into anyone from my class. Especially not Alex!

The Dobenhuber children were one big **imposition**. Vanessa **whinged** because she was hungry. Then Kai-Willem started **going on about** being thirsty, then moaned about stomach-ache. I decided simply to let it all go in one ear and out of the other.

Timmi spotted a boy from kindergarten and **abseiled** down the **climbing frame** with him. Then they both sat at the top and shouted mocking rhymes down to Vanessa and Deborah, who didn't dare to climb in their **Sunday best**.

I sat on the **bench** furthest away and felt fed up that I hadn't brought anything to read or at least my Walkman. I'd stay until six thirty, not a second longer.

What was Hille doing now? She was presumably lying in the swimming pool having a brilliant

---

imposition – Zumutung;
to whinge – sich beschweren;
to go on about – sich beschweren über etw.;
to abseil – abseilen;
climbing frame – Klettergerüst;
Sunday best – Sonntagskleidern;
bench – Bank

time whilst I was **stagnating** at the playground. And what if Alex were there?

The night before, I'd dreamed that he was kissing me. In primary school my friend Sabine, who was two years older, told me what happens when people who are in love kiss: they stick their tongues into each other's mouths. Sabine wanted to try it out there and then with me, and it made me feel really sick. But what would it be like with Alex?

I shut my eyes and felt Alex's hand touching my neck. "I've always fancied you," I heard him saying quietly. Just at that moment – when I was about to make him say something nice about my hair – I felt something cold, damp and **sludgy** on my back.

I turned round and saw Timmi and the other boy, both with **mud-smeared** hands and grinning faces. Deborah and Vanessa stood by, staring like the cows on Milka chocolate-bar wrappers.

"Are you **nuts**?" I **bellowed**. "We're going home right now. Timmi, I'll tell our parents, and you'll have TV banned for at least four weeks. And ..."

"I didn't do it," howled Timmi. "It was Benjamin, honest. He even wanted to smear the mud round your face."

Benjamin had planted himself in front of my brother. He was at least half a head taller than

---

to stagnate – versauern;
sludgy – schlammig;
mud-smeared – matschverschmierten;
nuts – wahnsinnig; to bellow – brüllen

Timmi. "Just don't you start telling lies!" he cried. "After all, it was your idea. You said your sister was stupid."

I wanted to say something more, but Timmi flung himself at Benjamin. I tried to separate the two **brawlers**, but Timmi suddenly had the energy he otherwise always lacked when it came to tidying his room.

"I'll tell my big brother," yelled Benjamin. Then he shouted for help so loudly that a few residents stuck their heads out of the windows and started **to get het up** about the disgraceful noise those children were making on a Sunday afternoon.

Deborah and Vanessa looked at me expectantly. "Are you going to beat them both up now?" Vanessa wanted to know. "Shall I help you?"

"I don't have to beat them up: they're doing it for themselves," I snapped at her.

"Benny, stop it!" I heard someone call.

I turned round. It was high time, too, that somebody sorted Benjamin out. Timmi had already pulled out some of his hair. Benny's brother came closer. The sky, previously full of thick clouds, had opened up and, blinded by the sun, I screwed up my eyes. Only when he was standing directly in front of me, did I **recognize** him.

"Carlo?!"

---

brawlers – Streithähne;
to get het up – sich aufregen;
to recognize – erkennen

With a practised grasp, he dragged his brother away from Timmi. “If you're not going to be sensible, we're going straight home.”

That worked. Benjamin ran back to the climbing frame, Timmi, Vanessa, Deborah and Kai-Willem behind him. Carlo plonked himself down on the bench next to me. He seemed to find it embarrassing to be seen at the playground with his little brother.

“There was a bit of trouble at home,” he said after a while. “My parents are **getting divorced**, and they're constantly arguing. So I took Benny out so that he doesn't hear all that stuff.”

“And I've **been landed with** some friends' children,” I said. “Though my brother would be quite enough to drive you mad all on his own.”

Carlo laughed. “Parents imagine that you like playing with younger brothers and sisters. But all they do is annoy you.” He was silent.

After a while he asked, “By the way, how are you getting on with going through the stuff for the school newspaper?”

I told him that, unfortunately, we hadn't done anything at all, and then we **slagged off** the teachers and school a bit, and wondered who we might get as our **form teacher** next year.

“Anyone but Nussler,” groaned Carlo. “Do you know what he got up to the other day?”

---

to get divorced – sich scheiden lassen;
to be landed with – aufs Auge gedrückt bekommen;
to slag off – schimpfen auf; form teacher – Klassenlehrer

But he never got to tell me because Deborah and Vanessa had fed grass to their little brother, and now he was feeling sick.

"I know what you have to do now," declared Deborah proudly. "You have to stick a finger down his throat."

After a quick consultation with Carlo, I decided that the grass hadn't done Kai-Willem any harm, and sent him off to play again.

"So tell me about Nussler …"

"Ah, right, yes. Well …"

When Kai-Willem urgently needed to wee, I looked at the clock and saw that it was already seven thirty. I gathered up the **brats** and set off for home. Carlo stayed behind.

"I'd rather wait until Benny's so tired that I can put him straight to bed," he said. "Then he'll not realize what's going on at home."

Only on the way home did it occur to me that I hadn't flirted with Carlo at all. And that would have been the ideal situation to practise and, what's more, I could have interrogated him about Alex. But on the other hand: the afternoon hadn't been all that bad either. Carlo had seemed much more cheerful than normal. He would be my new guinea pig.

---

brat – Balg

On Monday morning

Hille called for me as normal. "Hey," she said before I could **utter** a word. "Our argument was stupid, and I suspected you wrongly. I'm officially apologizing, and I've brought you something, too." She pulled a bar of chocolate out of her rucksack. "Just don't offer me any. I really do have to lose weight now. I've only eaten two peaches this morning."

I was, of course, pretty glad that the quarrel with Hille had ended. "So what did you do at the weekend?" I asked as we walked to the bus stop.

"I visited Gran," she said, grinning. "There was braised **beef** marinated in **vinegar** and **herbs** with **dumplings**, and cake in the afternoon. I told my mother I was going swimming with some people from our class. Oh well. But, you know, I really

---

to utter – sagen;
beef – Rindfleisch;
vinegar – Essig;
herbs – Kräuter;
dumpling – Knödel

would like to lose weight. My mother has bought me the most amazing dress, you see. It was ludicrously expensive, and we really can't afford that sort of thing."

She put her rucksack down and **raved** for at least five minutes about this dreamy thing in sky blue with a dark blue **pattern**, spaghetti **straps** and a rather **plunging neckline**. "There's just one problem," she said. "Just imagine, my mother ..."

"There'll be another problem in a minute," I interrupted her, "if we don't run, we'll miss our bus." We sprinted to the bus stop, but the bus had already gone.

"Fine, then we'll walk." Hille grinned at me. "You don't mind us being late, do you?"

I shook my head. I didn't want to **spoil** the good atmosphere with **trifles**.

"So why do you want to lose weight when you've got such a fabulous dress?" I asked her. "It'll look daft if it's too big."

Hille shook her head. "My mother bought it in a size too small. I even suspect her of doing it on purpose. The shop allegedly only had it in that size. I wore it for two minutes, but I couldn't **breathe out** or I'd have **burst** a **seam**." She looked

---

to rave – schwärmen;
pattern – Muster; strap – Träger;
plunging neckline – tiefer Ausschnitt;
to spoil – verderben;
trifle – Kleinigkeit;
to breathe out – ausatmen;
to burst – platzen; seam – Naht

so sad that I felt utterly sorry for her. But I had no idea how I could help her.

"By the way, I took your advice and applied for a job in a **butcher's** shop," said Hille after a while. "You know the branch in the pedestrian precinct? They're looking for someone to stuff sandwiches. That's my absolute nightmare job. Cutting up bread-rolls, stuffing them, selling them. Cutting up bread-rolls ..." She laughed. "And what am I going to do if they want me?"

"It's just practice," I reminded her. "By the way, I've decided to use Carlo as a guinea pig no matter what." I told her about my afternoon at the playground, and she thought I'd made the right decision.

In fact, it wasn't remotely worth going to school since most of the classes were cancelled because of the preparations for the big events: Open Day and the school party to round it all off. Kevin gave Hille and me the material for the school newspaper and said we could just as easily sort through it on our own.

Hille protested, but I **dug** her in the ribs and said with the most friendly smile, "But of course, we'll do it." I wanted absolutely nothing more to do with Kevin quite so soon.

---

butcher – Metzger;
to dig – stoßen

Probably fate **tipped** me **off** to get home earlier than usual that Monday. Even when I was only on the stairs, I was surprised to see that my bedroom door was wide open. Timmi was sitting at my desk, drawing.

I just said, "**Get lost**!" Then I noticed that he'd found something quite special to draw all over. My diary! He must have found the key which I'd hidden so well!

With a cry, I pounced on him, but he was quicker. With the diary pressed to his chest like a treasure, he rushed downstairs to seek protection – from Mum, of course.

I ran after him, but it was already too late. He had stuck the open diary under her nose and, guaranteed, she'd seen the last thing I wrote: *Alex, I love you!* I had written it with red **felt-tip** and had stuck gold stars around it.

I wrenched the book out of her hands. "That's my private life, it's got nothing to do with anyone else," I said as quietly as I could.

"I'm sorry, I didn't know it was your diary," she tried to explain herself. "There's no way I'd ever read your diary, you know that."

She looked at me. Even Timmi was quiet for a moment. He probably **sensed** that something important was going on and that he stood a greater chance of hearing it if he kept a low profile. But he

---

to tip off – einen Hinweis geben;
Get lost! – Verzieh dich!;
felt-tip – Filzstift; to sense – spüren

was mistaken. The subject was probably too controversial for her, too, because she just said that we'd have to talk about it some other time.

"I'll pay you back!" I threatened my brother as we climbed the stairs.

Timmi just grinned. "I know you're in love."

Before I could **give him a clout**, he'd run off into his bedroom. He opened the door cautiously a **crack**. "You and Carlo, you're in love with one another. Benny says so, too. The whole kindergarten knows already."

I stayed where I was. "Where'd you get that nonsense?"

"Benny said you two looked just as stupid as people in love films. Like this!" He rolled his eyes and pursed his lips.

If he was expecting me to give him a clout, he was mistaken. He could believe what he liked! The main thing was that he had no idea who I was really in love with.

I locked my bedroom door, sat in my rocking chair, and opened my diary. Hopefully, Mum hadn't seen what it said on the opposite page: *we kissed!!!!* Naturally she would immediately connect that with *Alex, I love you!* And yet it was all fantasy and dreams. Unfortunately!

I ran to the telephone; I just had to talk to Hille about it. But Mum was ringing a friend, and was just telling her that I was still pretty young for that

---

to give sb a clout – jmdm. eine scheuern;
crack – (hier) Spaltbreit

sort of thing and that she was still playing with dolls at my age.

What I wanted most was to fling open the sitting room door and tell her quite coolly that I simply stood more chance with boys than she did then. But I was probably better off standing outside the door and listening. I didn't feel in the slightest bit bad because at the end of the day, it was all about me.

For what must have been at least three minutes, I listened to the usual "yes, right … I'll do that … I think so, too" and so on. I had just decided to spare myself the rest of the phone call when I heard Mum saying that Alex was in my class, no two ways about it, and that she was wondering whether she shouldn't just contact his parents.

At that moment Timmi started **screaming blue murder** outside in the garden, and Mum immediately hung up to go and rescue her darling from some wild animal or other.

It was just a **wasp** that had **stung** his foot, but he made a huge performance until Mum promised to let him watch his three favourite programmes that afternoon.

"And a vanilla pudding," he demanded. "And no vegetables today."

She murmured something and laid him on the sitting room sofa. Then she switched the television on. She didn't seem to notice in the slightest

---

to scream blue murder – wie am Spieß schreien;
wasp – Wespe; to sting – stechen

that I was sitting motionless on the stairs the whole time.

I'd have had at least as much reason to howl as Timmi had. What if Mum were to ring the school and ask who Alex was? And what if she told his parents that we'd kissed? Would his parents then talk to him about it? There's no way Alex would have the faintest idea what they were talking about!

I felt hot and cold all over when I imagined it. It would be *the* sensation! The whole class – no, the whole school – would be laughing at me. Julia fantasizes that she's **snogging** Alex, and her parents believe it to boot. And he doesn't want to know a thing about her! Think of the way she looks! That strange hairstyle! I stood up and examined myself in the hall mirror.

Mum, a tub of vanilla pudding in her left hand and a cream for insect stings in her right, looked at me in astonishment. "Is something the matter?"

I nodded. "I think I'll have my hair cut again. Or I'll get myself a new hair colour. Or perhaps red **streaks** ..."

She shook her head in disbelief. "Julia, don't you have anything else to think about at the moment? Your brother's **in pain**, and all you can think about is your appearance. Are all teenagers

---

to snog – rumknutschen;
streak – Strähnchen;
to be in pain – Schmerzen haben

so **superficial**?" Then she ran into the living room to her darling Timmi.

I wished my whole family would just get lost. I decided I'd be better off doing something about my appearance than doing my homework. In the chemist's shop I bought some extra firm hair gel and a blue eyeliner. I didn't have enough pocket money left over that month to buy anything else. But by the time of the school party, I'd be able to afford a pink lipstick.

Then I went to Hille's. I desperately had to talk to someone sensible.

"Hille, you're not listening at all!"

My friend gave a start. "Yes, of course, I am, and I think it's pretty stupid, too, the way your mother's behaving, and that she then goes and tells her friends everything." She laughed wildly. "It's just that I've got an interview at the butcher's soon. Of course, I don't want the job at all, but I do want someone to want *me* at long last! And on top of that, we've got to do that stuff for the school newspaper. It's all so stupid."

For a moment I had the impression that she was about to **burst into tears**, but she pulled herself together again.

"So how did you come up with the daft idea of writing down your dream in the first place?" she asked.

---

superficial – oberflächlich;
to burst into tears – in Tränen ausbrechen

The dream was so wonderful, I could have replied. I will never forget it because it was the first time that I'd been kissed. It felt like standing in a meadow in spring, breathing in the air and feeling that you're very happy. I could have said all that, but I just shrugged my shoulders and gave an embarrassed grin.

"Anyway, I've now not just got the problem of keeping things going with Alex until the school party, but also that my parents must **under no circumstances** ring his home," I sighed.

"And I've got a big fat problem, too," grumbled Hille. "Time's gradually running out for me to find a holiday job. All the good jobs have already gone, guaranteed. Do you want me to list everything I've already done in order to find one?"

I shook my head. I'd have dearly loved to yawn. At that moment, I really couldn't give a toss about Hille's problems.

"I could just try taking a different route to school tomorrow," I wondered aloud. "Perhaps I'll be lucky and bump into Alex. In fact, I ought to warn him really about what he might be in for. Phone call from my mother and stuff!"

"So give it a go." Hille sounded pretty uninterested.

I strolled through town. I had no desire to go home. The conversation with Hille hadn't got me any further either. She did listen to everything,

---

under no circumstances – auf keinen Fall

but in truth she wasn't interested in anything except her stupid holiday job.

Maybe I'll bump into Alex, I mused, as I sat myself down on one of the benches by the Town Hall fountains. But that was, of course, pure wishful thinking. When a bus full of pensioners stopped in the nearby car park and the old **folk** rushed over to sit on the benches, I gave up. I decided to go home and do something for school. It was always a good idea to produce an orderly exercise book just before the teachers' marks meeting.

I almost stumbled over a bicycle trailer that was standing on the pavement.

"Sorry!" called someone from the front garden.

I was about to complain when I saw that it was Carlo who was delivering newspapers. He didn't seem to recognize me initially either because he seemed pretty embarrassed.

"I'll walk a bit of the way with you," I said to him. This time, I resolved, I'd find out something about Alex.

Carlo nodded. Once a week, so he told me, he delivered advertising leaflets for the supermarket, and if he was lucky, he'd be able to work there for two weeks in the holidays. "I just don't know what I'm going to do with my brother. The kindergarten's on holiday, and my mother finally **moved out** yesterday. Tell you what, families are pretty **tough**."

---

folk – Menschen;
to move out – ausziehen; tough – hart

"Too right. If you knew what I constantly have to put up with from my brother! You know, my parents act as if Timmi's the best thing since sliced bread and as for me, well, hey. I'm simply there, just like a piece of **furniture**."

Carlo pushed the bike, I **chucked** the leaflets into the letter boxes, and we talked as we did so: about our parents, our brothers, school ... Carlo was a really good listener. I'd have liked to tell him everything – about Alex, too – but in the end I didn't.

By late afternoon we'd finished our deliveries. Now I'll ask him if he wants to invite me for a hamburger in return for my help, I thought. It would be the ideal moment to practise my flirting!

Then Carlo said, shocked, that it was already very late and that he'd got to pick his brother up from a kindergarten friend's house.

Whatever, I thought; by now I'd come **to get on** so well **with** Carlo that I'd tell him about Alex sometime and then he'd help me. Of this much, I was quite sure: you can **rely** on Carlo.

Over supper I could tell by the way my parents were behaving that they'd been talking about my diary entry. I'd have loved to **lodge a complaint** with the child protection services or some **court** or other for this **snooping**.

---

furniture – Möbel; to chuck – werfen;
to get on with – sich mit jmdm. verstehen;
to rely – sich verlassen;
to lodge a complaint – sich beschweren; court – Gericht;
to snoop – schnüffeln

Timmi went to bed without any objections after supper. As of that moment, I had been warned. What had Mum and Dad promised him to make him go to bed without yelling and trying to spin it out for another half an hour for the first time in his life?

Dad cleared his throat and adopted his I-only-want-the-best-for-you expression. "Julia, I think we should talk."

I gave him a friendly smile. "That's what we spend all evening doing." Inside, I was **seething with anger**.

Dad cleared his throat once again and then said there really was no point **beating about the bush**. He and Mum were wondering whether I wasn't too young to be in a **relationship**.

"I'm not in a 'relationship' or whatever you call it!" Relationship: I hated that word. I wanted love, not a 'relationship'. But my parents would never understand that.

Mum laughed nervously. "Julia, the business with your diary was unfortunate, and I told you I was sorry. But you must admit that we have to say something about it – even though we only found out about it by chance. We don't want to **forbid** you to see Alex. But not that long ago it was still Kevin, and now Alex! Isn't it all happening a bit

---

to seeth with anger – vor Wut kochen;
to beat about the bush – drum herumreden;
relationship – Beziehung;
to forbid – verbieten

quickly?" She looked, annoyed, at Dad, who had meanwhile lit a cigarette.

"We don't want to forbid you to see Alex," repeated Dad, self-consciously extinguishing his cigarette. There's a **ban** on smoking in our house, and the fact that he'd lit a cigarette told me how nervous he was. "But we'd really like to meet him sometime. We don't know the first thing about him ..."

I don't know much about him either, unfortunately, I thought.

"... so maybe it's best if we get in touch with his parents," I heard Mum saying.

I sighed quietly. I had no choice: I had to tell them the truth, however embarrassing it may be.

"But there's nothing **real** about any of it," I said quietly. "I just dreamed the whole thing up, and I wrote it down because it was such a lovely dream."

Mum and Dad looked at one another. Mum shook her head. "We're pretty **broad-minded** when it comes to your behaviour, you know that. But lies, Julia: lies we won't tolerate. That destroys all the trust in the family."

It was enough to drive you mad. I told the truth and nobody believed me. Would I be better off lying in future? All the same, I managed to convince my parents that calling Alex's parents wasn't a good idea. I promised in return to bring him

---

ban – Verbot; real – wirklich;
broad-minded – tolerant

home with me soon so that they could convince themselves that he was harmless.

When I stood up, Mum held on to my arm. She made an effort to smile. "You know that you can always come to your parents if you've got a problem. And I got on well with Kevin, too, didn't I?"

I nodded.

In the sitting room I discovered Timmi in front of the television. He'd turned the volume right down and was watching an action film. I was initially about to run off to our parents and tell tales, but then it occurred to me that my brother could occasionally also be put to good use.

"Timmi, if you want to earn some money ..."

"'course I want to earn some money."

"You can sell me your Mickey Mouse comics," I suggested. "Ten comics for one euro. It's a great deal."

Timmi thought briefly. "Two euros!"

I shook my head. "Fine, then don't bother. But you won't earn one euro again that quickly, believe you me. When you've thought again, you can let me know."

I had to do something.

I sat at the desk gazing into space until I finally wrote Alex a love-letter which I then burnt. I'd never let any kind of evidence fall into my parents' hands again.

But I didn't feel any better afterwards either. I decided to ring Carlo and flirt on the phone with him. On the phone it was bound to work better and then – who knows: perhaps he'd tell me something about Alex, and then I could ring Alex.

"Hey, Carlo," I said after we'd chatted for ages about school and the school party, "d'you know that I really like you?"

My voice did sound a bit funny. I really don't see why, I thought; I'm not remotely bothered about him.

"Hello, are you still there?" I asked after a long pause.

Carlo cleared his throat. "What did you just say?"

I turned bright red with anger. What kind of ideas above his station was this guy getting? I'd have liked to **hang up** on him, but at the end of the day he was my guinea pig and maybe it was quite good after all that he hadn't reacted in the way I'd expected.

I thought briefly and decided to act naïve.

"I didn't say anything," I said. "Maybe there's interference on the line."

"It does sometimes happen that other people suddenly join in your conversation," said Carlo, and told me an interminable story about something that had once happened to his father.

"Wow, is it hot today," said Hille next morning at school.

She hadn't arrived at school until the third period because of a **dentist's** appointment, and I

---

to hang up – auflegen; dentist – Zahnarzt

had, in fact, hoped that some teacher would think of making Alex sit with me at the front, but Alex wasn't there.

"I don't know what's worse: dentist, or History with Napoleon," moaned my friend as Napoleon entered the classroom.

Eileen turned round. She said loudly: "Do you think the lesson'll be cancelled because of the heat?"

We were just wondering whether we should go to the head teacher and demand that classes be cancelled on account of the heat when Napoleon interrupted us. We were nothing but a coffee circle, he said, and in any case were always talking rubbish.

He gave a mean smile. "I still need oral marks from one of you. Shall I just see who it is?" He fished out his red notebook and put his glasses on.

"Oh God, it's my turn, I just know it is," moaned Hille next to me.

Napoleon had put his notebook on the desk and was looking straight in our direction. Hille would get an F, you could tell just by looking at her.

"Herr Dieringer," I said quickly, "I don't like you calling us a 'coffee circle'. We were discussing something interesting, you see." Napoleon raised his eyebrows. I had to be quick. "We were discussing the **offside rule**."

"Oh? I can't believe you know much about that!"

---

offside rule – Abseitsregel

Hille had got it. It would work. She had the expression of someone who had almost **drowned** and was **clutching at straws** to save herself.

"Oh yes, I do," she said, "but Julia and Jenny don't believe me."

"Oh, so let's have it," said Napoleon.

It worked. Five minutes later he had forgotten that he actually wanted to give out oral marks. Instead he stood at the blackboard using stick-figures to tell us how he played in the regional league thirty-five years ago and scored the winning goal in the 83rd minute. The referee had disallowed it for being offside, but it wasn't offside, as Napoleon was always telling us.

Of course, none of us was interested in that – we had heard this story at least three times over the last school year – but it was still better than having him orally test us on the first constitution of the French Revolution.

Napoleon was **struggling** with the stick-figures on the blackboard – he had miscounted and had drawn twenty-three – and we sat comfortably in our seats lost in our own thoughts.

"For Jenny," Miriam whispered behind me, and gave me a folded-up piece of paper.

I was all set to pass it on when Hille grinned at me. "Love letters are banned in class!" she whispered. "Let's see who fancies who!"

---

to drown – ertrinken; to clutch at straws – nach dem rettenden Strohhalm greifen; to struggle – kämpfen

However, it wasn't a love letter but an invitation to Jenny's birthday party. *The party*, Jenny had written, *has to be moved forward for technical reasons, and is taking place tonight from 6.30 pm.* She had in the meantime invited seven girls and four boys from our class, and most of them had accepted.

Hille grinned at me. "Alex isn't here today, that's why he's not on the list. But I know for a fact that's he's invited. And what about us?"

I shrugged my shoulders. Of course, I was annoyed that Jenny hadn't invited me to her party, but I'd never have admitted it.

"Jenny's forgotten about us, no doubt," said Hille quietly. "But we're going, what do you reckon?"

Before I could protest she'd put our names on the list and had drawn a huge OK next to them. With an **innocent** smile she tapped Jenny on the shoulder and handed her the piece of paper.

Jenny and Eileen studied the list. Then they both turned round.

"Someone must have cut the bottom half off," said Jenny. "Your names were on there. Though I'd still have let you know in any case."

"'Course you would," I said, having to **suppress** a grin.

"Psst!" someone said at the back.

Napoleon had a **bad-tempered** look. "You're

---

innocent – unschuldig; to suppress – verkneifen; bad-tempered – missmutig not in the slightest bit interested in what you're being told," he growled. "Where were we? Oh yes, electoral law in the First Constitution!"

He swept round and wiped the twenty-three little red and green men off the blackboard with a dripping sponge. Then he produced his notebook, picked on Alex, realized that he wasn't there, and **announced** that there would be a short test next lesson.

At lunchtime I wished Hille lots of luck with her interview at the butcher's. "It'll all go fine for you," I said hopefully, "and for me, too."

She looked at me inquiringly. "You mean this evening?"

"Yes," I said. "I'll know one way or the other this evening. I'm quite sure of it! Hille, I'll never forget you just inviting us. Brilliant!"

Jenny had absolutely no choice but to act as if we'd been invited. I'd asked her at the main break whether we needed to bring a horror film, too, but she said she already had three and there wouldn't be enough time as it was.

"I'll call for you," I promised Hille and went home happier than I'd been for ages.

Of course, Jenny was the most important person at her party, but somehow I had to be able to work things so that I could get to talk to Alex. I thought it was boring to ask him about his time in America. He'd probably been over all that a thousand

---

to announce – ankündigen

times already. But there had to be some topic that really interested him. Football? Tennis? Music? I realized that my good mood was evaporating. I'd probably just sit there and not say a word, and Jenny would be chatting away to Alex, laughing and …

The comics! Of course! Why didn't I think of it sooner? I rushed into the house and offered Timmi two euros for his comics. Then I grabbed the telephone. Now I had a good reason to ring Alex.

I had to let it ring at least ten times before anyone finally answered. My heart beat more loudly with every ring.

"Cleef," said Alex.

"Hello, it's Julia. From your class," I added.

He gave a short laugh. "I know. I recognized you straight away. I felt sick this morning, that's why I didn't come to school. But I'm fine again now."

"I've got quite a lot of comics from my brother," I said quickly before an embarrassing pause could develop. "If you're coming to Jenny's party tonight, I'll bring them with me."

"Comics? Mickey Mouse?"

"Ten of them. They're in fantastic condition."

"Julia, you're brilliant. Yes, that's a great idea. Don't forget the comics, will you?"

"Julia, you're brilliant!" he'd said to me. I wrote that sentence in my diary in gold pen. Then I informed my mother that I'd been invited to a schoolfriend's birthday party that evening, and cleared everything out of my wardrobe.

It was no good. I needed something new to wear. I went into town armed with my birthday money and bought myself a silver-grey **sparkly** top and the pink lipstick that I couldn't in fact afford, and an illustrated book about dolphins for Jenny which was reduced. Then I spotted some **obscenely expensive wrapping paper** with little coloured hearts, and decided to wrap Alex's comics in it. If he was shocked, I could always say that I couldn't find any other paper.

Extremely satisfied, I was home shortly after half four. I still had plenty of time to wash my hair, get changed and put my make-up on. But first I wanted to wrap my presents.

"Timmi," I called, "could you bring me the comics now?"

My brother appeared at the top of the stairs. He was smirking. "I'm not as stupid as you think! The comics are **worth** loads more than that."

I would dearly have loved to **shake** him, but I didn't want to spoil my mood. And, what's more, Mum was in the **vicinity**. I could hear her opening the living room door.

"Okay, fine, I'll give you three euros!" I raised my offer. "But that really is your lot."

"Julia!" Mum was standing in the hallway giv-

---

sparkly – glänzend;
obscenely expensive – sündhaft teuer;
wrapping paper – Geschenkpapier;
worth – wert;
to shake – schütteln;
vicinity – Nähe

ing me a **reproachful** look. "I don't want you doing business with your brother. And what's more ..."

"If Timmi and I want to do business, then it's nothing to do with anyone but us," I said very loudly.

Timmi was still grinning. He fished a ten euro note from out of his trouser pocket and waved it around under my nose. "That's what I got!"

"Good for you," I said unkindly. "Are you selling me your comics now or not?"

"They've already been sold," said Timmi happily. "I got ten euros for them."

I had to sit down. Mum looked at me, concerned.

"Who did you sell the comics to?"

Mum sent Timmi to his room and brought me a glass of water. "You'd just gone out when a boy came. He said you were from his class and that you'd offered him the comics. And he gave Timmi ten euros for them. I must say, I thought it was a bit too much, but Timmi made a lot of fuss and ... well, you know what that means."

"Yes," I murmured. "I know." Slowly, I climbed the stairs to my bedroom.

An hour later I had to some extent recovered. Maybe it wasn't so bad that Alex had collected the comics himself. Maybe he'd even hoped to see me. My mood suddenly improved again. In any case, I

---

reproachful – tadelnd

now had a topic of conversation: we could slag my brother off for having got too much money out of him, and I could invite Alex for an ice cream to make up for it.

At ten to six, Hille rang the bell like mad.

"Wow, look at the state of you!" I said when I opened the door for her.

"D'you think you'd look any better if you'd just spent three quarters of an hour buttering bread-rolls like on a production line? Here!" She held out her **bandaged** thumbs to me. "I almost **hacked** my fingertips **off**. **Slice** the sausage, slice the bread-roll open, stick the sausage in, pickled gherkin on top, close it up and so on ... I mean, honestly!"

Hille was so fed up that I fetched some ice cream from the chest freezer and heaped a gigantic portion onto a plate for us. We'd earned it now. Hille didn't say another word about her diet either.

When she'd eaten it up, she just said, "Would you like my new dress? It doesn't matter if it's too big, does it?"

I shook my head. I'd just had a brilliant idea. "Why exactly do you have to be made to fit the dress?" I asked her. "What do you say to us trying to make the dress fit you?"

My friend looked at me inquiringly, then she roared with laughter. "You mean ...?"

---

bandaged – verbunden;
to hack off – abschneiden;
to slice – schneiden

"Precisely! I'll help you – you probably can't do it alone, what with your thumbs. Best thing is for us to start first thing tomorrow. If it doesn't work out with the job, then we'll just find another kind of success," I said giggling. "But we'd better go now. I'm allowed to stay until ten. What about you?"

"I don't really feel like going to Jenny's party any more. I'd most like to go home and watch TV or alter my dress."

"We'll do that tomorrow for sure," I promised her. "But you have to come with me. I'll feel better if you do, okay?"

Somehow ...

I managed to persuade Hille to come with me. Since she'd forgotten her present – a dark blue glass vase – we had to **drop by** her house first, and we were the last to turn up at Jenny's.

Jenny had cleared out the living room and had laid out normal and camping mattresses, on which most kids were sitting **cross-legged**, eating pizza with chocolate spread. The **blinds** were almost completely shut. I tried **to get my bearings** in the semi-darkness.

"Come and sit with us," cried Miriam. "There's still tons of pizza left. We'll burst if we carry on eating."

Hille gave a tortured laugh. The evening was going to be difficult for her.

---

to drop by – bei jmdm. vorbeigehen;
cross-legged – im Schneidersitz;
blind – Rollladen;
to get my bearings – sich zurechtfinden

"Can you see Alex anywhere?" I asked her in a whisper.

Hille screwed up her eyes. "Not so far," she said, "but maybe he's on his way."

We sat down by Miriam, Rita and Diniah and discovered that Jenny's mother had mistakenly ordered 30 pizza bases with chocolate spread instead of 20.

"They've all got to be eaten up now," said Diniah, pulling a face. "I'm sure I'll never eat chocolate spread ever again in my whole life."

The atmosphere was pretty **indifferent**. Jenny spent the whole time running around, **unwrapping** presents and thanking everyone effusively.

The chocolate pizza had fallen onto Eileen's pale blue dress. She was trying to wash the mark out, but **to no avail**. A couple of the boys were playing cards; Jenny's cousin was putting CDs on that most people thought were stupid; and only Hille seemed to be having a good time.

"I've not eaten chocolate pizza **for yonks and yonks**," she declared, her mouth full. "My mother always says nobody could possibly eat it."

I stood up and wandered through the room. Jenny's cousin had finally chosen a good CD, and a couple of girls were dancing in the hallway.

Eileen and Jenny were standing outside the kitchen looking rather at a loss.

---

indifferent – mäßig; to unwrap – auspacken;
to no avail – ohne Erfolg;
for yonks and yonks – seit Ewigkeiten

"Should I call him?" I heard Jenny saying. "He did promise to come. He ought really to have been here ages ago."

She had spotted me and **exchanged** brief looks with her friend. I could almost have grinned. The two of them couldn't **fool** me.

"Alex told me on the phone that he was definitely coming," I said quite **casually**. I'd dearly love to have added: he also said he thought I was brilliant. But it was Jenny's birthday party, and I didn't want to spoil the atmosphere too much for her.

"Well then, presumably he'll still turn up," she said. "Why don't we start with the videos now? My parents will be back at eleven thirty, and then the party's over, unfortunately. Andreas, could you just stick the video in?"

We sat around the television in a semi-circle, Jenny let the blinds right down, warned us not to scream too hysterically during the horror film because we'd get into trouble from the other **tenants** in the building, and gave the **go-ahead**.

Nothing happened.

Hille giggled. "Won't work," she said. "The video machine's definitely had it. We had the same problem not long ago."

Someone turned the ceiling light on so that And-

---

to exchange – austauschen;
to fool – täuschen;
casually – locker;
tenant – Mieter;
go-ahead – Startzeichen

reas, who was fumbling around with the video recorder, his face bright red, could see something.

"He doesn't know anything about technology," cried Norman, and within a few minutes five people were crowded around the video recorder pressing every conceivable button – to no avail.

"I'll ring Alex," Jenny suddenly said. "Hundred percent certain Alex will know what to do." She stood up and ran to the telephone.

I was a hundred percent certain that she was thrilled to have a reason to ring him. On the one hand, **it served her right** that he hadn't come; on the other hand I hoped that he'd still turn up. I'd immediately tell him how awful my brother's behaviour had been, and that I'd like to invite him for an ice cream to make up for it.

Meanwhile a big fight had broken out in the living room about which of the three videos that Jenny had got to watch first.

"First off we've got to get this pile of junk working," cursed Rita, who was pressing all the buttons like mad and checking that everything was plugged in. "I'm only allowed to stay until half nine, and if we don't start, it won't be worth it any more anyway."

"So?" she then called to Jenny, who was standing in the doorway holding the phone. "Is Alex coming?"

My heart beat quite violently. He was bound to come. After all, he'd told me only this afternoon

---

it serves sb right – das geschieht jmdm. recht

how brilliant he thought I was. He simply had to come.

Jenny shook her head. She seemed completely frustrated. "I spoke to his mother. He's still not feeling completely better. He's in bed reading comics."

"He's reading comics?"

Everyone looked at me in astonishment. I must have said it out loud.

"So?" said Eileen aggressively. "What's wrong with that? So Alex likes comics. In America that's what adults do, too. I'm sure they're far more interesting to read than books about dolphins and stuff."

Alex was lying in bed reading the comics he'd bought from my brother. I didn't know whether to laugh or to cry.

"Well?" Hille gave me a nudge. "D'you want to stay, or shall we go?"

"Let's go," I said. "We're not such good friends with Jenny that we have to spend the whole evening hanging around here."

"I'm inviting you for a pizza," said Hille as we made our way home.

"Pizza? I couldn't even look at another pizza."

"Proper pizza. Margarita or pepperoni or something. I need something real after all that sweet stuff."

She was right. A jar of pickled gherkins would have done the trick, but if Hille absolutely insisted. We ordered two slices of pizza from the kiosk in Königstraße.

"You know what?" said my friend, biting into her pizza with **relish**. "I'm just not going to be part of **this whole palaver** any more. I don't absolutely have to have a holiday job. I just wanted to buy some new things to wear because I've been hoping to be mega thin by the start of the next school year. But that just doesn't seem to work for me. Hey, isn't that Carlo over there?" She pointed with her finger to the other side of the road. "Is he delivering newspapers?"

I nodded. "He's got a job. And he's got a lot of problems at home. His parents are getting divorced. You know, just the usual stuff. Stress with his little brother and so on."

"What do you think of him?"

"Who? The little brother? Carlo?"

"Carlo, of course!"

I thought for a moment. What did I actually think of Carlo?

"Nice," I said after a moment's hesitation. "In fact, he's incredibly nice. He listens to you, thinks about it, and ... so he's just nice. Shall I get you a Coke?"

Hille seemed to wonder whether or not to wave to Carlo, but then decided against it. "Can't you fall in love with him?" she asked. "He's much more normal than Alex."

"Fall in love with Carlo?" I laughed out loud. "Carlo's a good friend; you can tell him pretty

---

relish – Genuss;
the whole palaver – das ganze Theater

much anything, but I can't fall in love with him. I'm simply nuts about Alex, got it?"

Hille nodded, but I don't think she understood. "So what's going to happen next?"

"Of course, I'd pinned all my hopes on this evening," I said hestitantly. "But there's still the school party." I didn't want to ruin Hille's good mood.

She smiled at me. "You'll manage it, **dead cert**. Eileen and Jenny don't stand a chance against you, believe me."

"Wow, Julia, am I glad that we managed it," Hille greeted me the following morning.

It had taken us nearly an hour and a half to let out her dress. She could finally put it on without having to hold her breath.

"Brilliant," I said and was truly **blown away**. "Hille, that looks fantastic on you."

At school the usual stress prior to school fêtes ruled the day. Our class's job was to put up posters all over the town inviting everyone to the Open Day and school party.

"And in this heat," moaned Eileen. "Do we all have to do it?"

"All of you," said Napoleon. "Or we'll do some more French Revolution." He had, in fact, intended to set a test for this lesson. However, he didn't mention it further. Perhaps he was glad, too, that he didn't have to mark any of our work.

---

dead cert – ganz bestimmt; blown away – hingerissen

"You can go around in groups of four. Take the posters and some sticky tape, and make sure you ask politely before sticking one up," he impressed upon us.

Hille gave me a meaningful look. Then she moved her head almost **imperceptibly** in Alex's direction.

I'd got it. But how could I manage to get into the same group as him? I **didn't have the foggiest**. And, what's more, Eileen, Jenny and Rita had immediately turned to him and called that he could go with them. He had simply nodded.

Right before the first period started, I'd **made a beeline for** him together with Hille and I'd told him that my brother had totally **ripped him off**. He had just laughed and had said that the comics were in such good condition that they were in any case worth what he'd paid for them, and that I really didn't have to worry about it. I'd just been about to suggest – so relaxed had I become by that point – inviting him for an ice cream when he remembered that he'd forgotten to lock up his bike. With an "Oh, my God, I hope no one's **nicked** it" he'd left Hille and me standing there.

Everything seemed to be going wrong again. Hille, Carlo and I made a **threesome** – without

---

imperceptibly – unmerklich;
to not have the foggiest – keine blassen Schimmer haben;
to make a beeline for sb – schnurstracks auf jmdn. zugehen; to rip sb off – jmdn. ausnehmen;
to nick – klauen;
threesome – Dreiergruppe

Anne: she'd **ducked out** because she wasn't feeling very well.

"Now is the big moment," cried Napoleon, planting himself in front of the desk. "I've written a list of the roads where the posters are going. Unfortunately, I didn't reckon on it being so hot today. But one group's in luck: they'll be going to the swimming pool area with lots of trees, a park and a stream. The others will just have to put something on their heads so they don't get **sunstroke.**"

"Swimming pool, swimming pool," a few people shouted at first, followed by practically the whole class.

Napoleon shook his head. "The threesome gets the swimming pool area. It's unfair otherwise, don't you see?"

Hille and I beamed at one another as we went up to the front desk to collect our posters. Alex not being there only bothered me marginally.

"You're lucky," said Eileen. She sounded pretty jealous. "And we have to **traipse** around the industrial estate in this hideous heat. I feel sick already."

"But there are four of you," said Hille in our **defence.**

"Do you want to **swap**?" I asked. The idea had

---

to duck out – abspringen;
sunstroke – Sonnenstich;
to traipse – latschen;
defence – Verteidigung;
to swap – tauschen

occurred to me quite spontaneously that I might be able to join Alex's group.

Hille stared at me, horrified. "Swap?" she asked in surprise. "**Are you kidding**? Why should we swap?"

"Well, you know," I said, "if someone from the other group joins us, we'll be finished sooner, even if we have to walk round in the sun." The argument was, it's true, pretty **feeble**, but I didn't care at that moment. The main thing was that Hille had got it.

"It's true," she said decisively. "Julia's right. So you can do our **shady** trip – but only as a threesome!"

Eileen, Jenny and Rita looked at one another, undecided.

"It's fine," said Alex. "I don't mind the sun. We lived in Louisiana and I'm used to the heat. What do you reckon, Carlo?"

I looked at Carlo. For the first time in ages I looked at him more closely. *He* had blue eyes, too, I was astonished to realize. I'd spent hours chatting to him, and I'd never noticed that he had blue eyes. I smiled at him pleadingly and he nodded.

"So? Are you satisfied?" Hille asked quietly as we made our way outside.

"I'll never forget that you did that," I said. "Could you possibly talk to Carlo a bit? He's incredibly nice, you can have brilliant conversations

---

Are you kidding? – Machst du Witze?;
feeble – schwach; shady – schattig

with him. And have you ever noticed what lovely eyes he's got?"

Hille laughed. "Is it Alex you're in love with, or is it Carlo? Fine, I can certainly take care of him."

Poor Hille. It was at least thirty-three degrees in the shade, and she was wearing a long skirt whilst I just had a pair of shorts and a crop top on. It must have been a huge **sacrifice** for her **to pass up on** the pleasant poster trip to the swimming pool.

For a while we walked along as a foursome, slagging off the posters that our art teacher had devised with Year Five.

"Ouch," cried Hille at some point, holding onto Carlo, her face **distorted** with pain. "I've somehow twisted my **ankle**," she explained. "First of all the **mishap** with my thumb, and now my foot as well! But it's not that bad. I'll just sit down for a moment. You lot can go on ahead."

"... and do a bit of work," she added when Alex shook his head and said that, of course, we'd wait until she was feeling better again.

"Carlo can stay just in case I need the **emergency doctor**," she said, looking deadly serious. "And Julia and Alex have to go and put up some posters."

I took the pack of **poisonous** green posters from her. "Thanks," I whispered.

---

sacrifice – Opfer;
to pass up on – auf etw. verzichten;
distorted – schmerzverzerrt;
ankle – Fußgelenk; mishap – Pech;
emergency doctor – Notarzt; poisonous – giftig

"No problem," she whispered back. "See you this afternoon."

I marched through the industrial estate next to Alex. Lots of little businesses had **set up** there in the last few years, mostly consisting of just two or three containers.

"**Dismal**," is how Mum had described the industrial estate to a friend, "absolutely dismal."

But walking next to Alex, I'd have thought that absolutely anywhere was seventh heaven. For one thing I was really **chuffed** that he wasn't out with Eileen or Jenny, and secondly it was simply a great feeling to be so close to him.

I asked him why he **was** so **into** reading comics, and he told me. Whatever he said didn't matter to me. The only thing that mattered was hearing the sound of his voice.

"Oh dear," he said quite loudly after a while. "Now I've told you what happens in at least four comics. Did you notice anything?"

I gave a start. "Nah, should I have?"

"Those stupid posters! We're supposed to be putting posters up, not just going for a walk." He thought briefly. "What d'you reckon? Should we simply chuck them in the nearest litter bin? I reckon nobody in this industrial estate is going to come to our Open Day or to the school party either – guaranteed."

---

to set up – errichten; dismal – trostlos; chuffed – glücklich; to be into sth – sich für etw. interessieren

He gave me such a lovely smile that I had no choice. "Yes," I said.

Alex carefully rolled the posters up and pointed to the green waste paper bin directly opposite the bus stop. "No one will notice, take my word for it! He went over, whistling, stuffed the package into the bin and ran back to me. "Let's go for an ice cream now, what d'you reckon?"

I could have yelled with happiness. Alex and I were going for an ice cream! It was a dead cert: I'd turn up at the school party with him. Eileen and Jenny and absolutely everyone wouldn't believe their eyes. No two ways about it: none of them would ever have thought me capable of getting Alex.

He took my arm. "I reckon we'd better take those two in front of us." He gesticulated towards Hille and Carlo, who were still sitting on a little wall at the same street corner and waving to us.

I nodded graciously. As I'd soon have Alex all to myself, Hille and Carlo could come to the ice-cream café with us, no worries.

Hille remained firm. "I don't like ice cream," she declared, just drinking mineral water. "Were you successful?"

Alex laughed. "Yes, of course, we **coped with** it brilliantly. The whole industrial estate is covered in posters. People will be besieging our school, you just can't imagine it."

I felt rather bad when I thought about the

---

to cope with – mit etw. umgehen

posters in the litter bin, but maybe Alex was right and we'd have gone to all that effort for nothing anyway.

We were sitting outside and I'd put my sunglasses on. Partly because the sun really was blinding, but the second reason was much more important: I'd find it easier to flirt with Alex with my sunglasses on. I asked him very casually whether he liked being in our class.

Alex laughed. Then he got his sunglasses – mirrored ones! – from his rucksack. He grinned and said he'd had very **sensitive** eyes recently. Then he put them on and said that, of course, he liked being in our class.

He leant over to me. "The main reason is the great girls here," he said in an undertone.

I felt myself going red. Did he mean me? I desperately tried to find a good answer, but I simply couldn't think of anything.

Hille gave a low laugh and Carlo smiled, but I could clearly see that the pair felt **surplus** to requirements. At any rate, Carlo seemed to be very happy when Alex quite suddenly said goodbye and disappeared.

He'd barely gone when Hille jumped up. "Damn!" She didn't give a minute's thought to her **alleged** twisted foot. "Alex took my house key by mistake, the stupid **plonker**," she groaned. "I'll just run after him. Could you pay for me, Julia?"

---

sensitive – empfindlich; surplus – überflüssig; alleged – angeblich; plonker – Blödmann

Carlo and I were left sitting opposite one another. He wasn't wearing sunglasses, so I took mine off, too.

"What's wrong?" I asked. "You've got a really funny expression on your face, so ... sad."

"Sad?" Carlo shrugged his shoulders. "Sorry, I don't want to spoil the atmosphere. But sometimes **things just don't work out** the way you imagined they would." He looked straight at me and it somehow gave me a funny feeling. He smiled, but it was a sad smile. Presumably he was having **strife** with his parents again.

"Hey, Carlo, it'll all sort itself out," I said and wondered whether I should tell him about Alex and me. I remembered the stuff about the posters again. I felt absolutely terrible. I simply had to confess to someone!

"I have to tell you something," I said slowly.

He looked at me expectantly.

"Alex lied. It's not true that we stuck the posters up. We just stuffed them in a waste paper bin," I admitted. "Do you think that's awful?"

For a while he didn't say anything at all.

I could hear a young couple arguing at the next table, a mobile ringing somewhere, and a couple of schoolchildren running along the pavement, **squealing**.

"Say something, Carlo, please."

He shrugged his shoulders. "Mhm. I don't know.

---

things just don't work out – es läuft nicht;
strife – Ärger; to squeal – kreischen

I mean, I don't think it's good because ... well, the others are working and we're doing **stuff all**. Was it Alex's idea?"

I didn't say anything.

He laughed shortly. "You don't have to tell me. Alex is nice, I like him a lot, but he takes some things incredibly lightly. When I told him my mother had moved out, he just said we'd have more space at home now."

"Alex is just ... different!" I couldn't think of a better word.

Carlo nodded. He moved the vase of flowers from the middle of the table to the side and back again.

"Why are you so nervous?" I asked.

"I don't like the business about the posters," he said. "The others are relying on us doing our bit, and instead we're sitting in the café and ..."

"Fine!" I nodded. "I said yes when Alex asked me if we should chuck the posters in the bin. But you're right. It's somehow not really okay. So I'll run off now and **retrieve** the posters and go and stick them up."

"I'll come with you," said Carlo. "We'll do it together."

"I do think it's incredibly nice of Carlo to have helped you," said Hille when I rang her that evening and told her everything. "Alex is pretty chaotic. He doesn't **mean** any harm, but some-

---

stuff all – gar nichts; to retrieve – holen; to mean – vorhaben times I do find him annoying. But he's very good looking to make up for it."

Oh no, I thought, Hille's smitten, too. But *she* would be no competition for me. Firstly because we're friends, secondly because I fell for him first, and thirdly …

"Why aren't you saying anything?" she wanted to know. "I asked you what's going to happen next with you two."

"On Open Day I'm selling cakes with Alex from ten till twelve," I said. "After I'd stuck the posters up, I went back to school because Carlo said that the lists were already up. It was a fantastic tip. I put your name down, too. You can sell sandwiches from eleven till one."

"Are you kidding?" Hille was mightily fed up. "I hate sandwiches. I got a letter from the butcher's today. They offered to let me do work experience for them. They said I should come three afternoons in the holidays and stuff sandwiches."

"Well, it's better than no job at all," I said.

Hille should just stop making such a fuss. Instead of being glad that the roundabout technique finally helped her to get a holiday job, she just whinges about it.

"You don't seem to have understood me properly." Her voice sounded as if she were on the point of throwing something at the wall. "I'll just read you what these idiots say. **Hang on** a minute."

---

to hang on – warten

She put the receiver down and I heard paper rustling. "Doesn't matter," I cried. "Just tell me what was in it." But she couldn't hear me.

I clamped the telephone between my shoulder and my ear, and opened my wardrobe in the meantime. What could I wear for the school party? Maybe I should go to town and buy something else? Something in white, for example. That would go well with my blonde hair. And, above all, with Alex's eyes!

"Right, I'm going to read to you." Hille's voice **quivered** with rage. "First off there's a blah blah blah bit that goes on forever, as you always get in these letters, and then here it comes: *I am sure you will understand that we are unable to pay you for your work experience. However, you are most welcome to take one of our delicious, well-filled sandwiches home with you. Please do get in touch with us*. Blah, blah, blah. Even my mother says that's a bit much."

I realized that under the circumstances I could not expect Hille to sells sandwiches at school. I suggested that she just sell cakes with Alex and me.

"The school newspaper!" I went boiling hot as I suddenly remembered about it. "Hakan and Diana have signed up to photocopy everything and then to stick it all together. And the two of us have got to choose the articles!"

Damn, we were really **in for it**. Some kids in our

---

to quiver – zittern;
to be in for it – Ärger zu bekommen

class had managed to **woo** advertisers, only Hille and I were yet again not on track ...

She pacified me. "It's all fine. I sorted it out yonks ago. I foisted all the material onto Markus because he's always so well organized. He's given the stuff to Alex in the meantime."

"Alex!" I said. "And you think he's going to do it?"

Our school holds an Open Day once a year. And it's always the same. First of all the choir sings some welcome songs, then the head teacher gives a little speech, then the visitors are sent round all the rooms.

On this day, there are incredibly friendly teachers standing around everywhere, wanting to explain everything to anyone they can get their hands on. Even Strobel, our Chemistry teacher, who normally wears brown **cords**, wears a suit and a white shirt on Open Days and looks educationally **valuable** in a way he never manages for the whole of the rest of the school year.

The classrooms had been cleaned and the assembly hall had been freshly **painted**. So that nobody could see how **defaced** some of the desks were, we'd pushed them together and had covered them with tablecloths.

Hille and I set up the cake stall without Alex.

---

to woo – umwerben; cords – Kordhosen;
valuable – wertvoll; to paint – malen, streichen;
to deface – beschmieren

"I've just got to sort something out," he'd murmured and had quickly disappeared.

At around **half ten** the **onslaught** began. The queues for our cake counter became longer and longer.

Where on earth was Alex? Maybe he had simply dropped out? I was starting to become fed up when I spotted him. He was carrying two enormous **bunches of** wild **flowers** in his arm and was desperately searching for a vase.

"Looks much nicer," he said as he finally put the flowers next to the till. "Is there anything I can do to help?"

It was simply impossible to be angry with Alex. Hille did get at him a bit, but she wasn't really angry either.

We were just sharing out a chocolate cake when there was a sudden harsh flash. Hille dropped the rest of her cake. "Wow, that shocked me," she managed, her mouth full. She wiped her hand across her lips. "What would you like?" Hille asked a young woman in a grey trouser suit who was carrying a camera.

"Well," said the woman. "More photos." She laughed. "I'm Sabine Deries from the *Picture Press* agency. In fact, I only came because my son's in Year Seven and was absolutely desperate for me to take a few pictures."

---

half ten (eigentlich: half past ten) – halb elf;
onslaught – Ansturm;
bunch of flowers – Blumenstrauß

I rolled my eyes. Chatty Mummy: we all knew her type. She'd presumably go on to tell us that her son's spectacularly good at German and Maths, and ...

"**To cut a long story short**," the woman said, "I'm looking for a model for a magazine photo series." She hesitated for a moment. "The topic is: 'you can stuff your beanpoles.' The kind of girl I need has to be cheerful and quite **plump**. Do you think you might be interested? You'd be well-paid," she added, as she saw Hille's **dumbfounded** face.

"You mean me?" asked Hille. "Unbelievable! Of course. I'll do it at once. In fact, it's exactly what I've been looking for."

Hille was in seventh heaven. After she'd sorted everything out with Frau Deries, she gobbled the next piece of cake. "Now I'm eating for professional reasons, so to speak." She giggled. "Wow, how freaked out do you reckon my mum will be when I appear in the papers?"

"I reckon," said Hille as she called for me that evening on the way to the school party, "you simply have to **bide your time** until you're lucky. All those job applications, all that frustration, I could have saved myself all that. Fate had planned another career for me as a photo model."

---

to cut a long story short – kurz und gut;
plump – rundlich; dumbfounded – entgeistert;
to bide your time – abwarten

She was wearing her new dress and was madly proud and happy. She'd barely put any make-up on because Frau Deries had told her that she was looking for a natural-looking girl.

"And I shouldn't lose any weight for heaven's sake. She said so at least three times," Hille added with satisfaction. "My mother couldn't believe it. Tomorrow lunchtime she's finally going to cook something **proper** again. Spinach pasta bake, perhaps. D'you fancy coming?"

I shook my head. "You know I'm not that keen on spinach bake."

I didn't **begrudge** Hille her success, honestly. Perhaps it really was best just to bide your time. In her case it had led to a job as a model, even if only for the North Bavarian *Farmers' Weekly*. But all the same! Frau Deries had said the series would be sure to lead to further offers, and my friend could already half see herself in New York.

"I'll just let things with Alex **take their course**," I said. But I'll grab absolutely any opportunity that presents itself to me, I added to myself.

I didn't have much choice either. After putting both bunches of flowers on the table, Alex simply disappeared and I hadn't had any other opportunity to arrange to meet him tonight. Strangely enough, it suddenly didn't seem to bother me that much.

---

proper – richtig; to not begrudge sb sth – gönnen; to let sth take its course – etw. auf sich zukommen lassen

Hille had only not complained about Alex not being there because she'd been discovered as a model and in any case she hadn't really **taken in** anything that was going on around her.

To make up, for it, she'd promised to help me with my make-up and had brought her Indian silver jewellery with her.

"The necklace suits you fantastically," she said, **propelling** me towards the mirror. "I've brought three different coloured lipsticks with me, too. We'll just try them out and see what looks best."

Hille giggled as she painted my lips. "It's a bit like spreading stuff on bread-rolls. Ah well," she added when she saw my horrified face, "the goods sell better if they look good. That's what the woman in the butcher's said. And she was right, too."

I didn't want to fall out with my friend. I wanted to be beautiful and to appeal to Alex and the whole class would see that he and I …

"Ow," growled Hille. "Damn, I'll have to start all over again."

Timmi had slipped almost noiselessly into my room and had **pinched** her. He danced around us making Red Indian whooping noises.

"**Get lost**!" I barked at him.

"Timmi, come downstairs," called Mum from down below, "leave the girls in peace!"

"I've not told Julia yet that a man rang," he said

---

to take sth in – etw. wahrnehmen; to propel – schieben; to pinch – zwicken; get lost – verschwinde

as I pushed him out of the door. "But now I've told you. Do I get a reward? One euro?"

For a moment my heart almost stopped. Alex! It was bound to be Alex who'd rung! I looked down at my mother who was staring up expectantly. She was presumably wondering the same as I was.

"Oh yes?" I said, trying to make my voice sound as uninterested as possible. "So who rang, then?"

Timmi seemed to sense the **tension**. "What do I get for telling you?" he wanted to know.

"A box on the ears!" Hille rolled her eyes. Come on, let's carry on, she signalled to me.

Mum was just as much **on tenterhooks** as I was. She had, in the meantime, come upstairs and **crouched down** next to Timmi. "That's not fair of you," she said deliberately slowly. "You have to tell your sister now who rang." And me, too, she seemed to add to herself.

Meanwhile Timmi had started to feel **unsure** of himself. He was probably afraid of Mum's **strict** voice because he suddenly started crying and said he couldn't remember at all. Maybe he'd just seen it all on TV, he said, and he finally wanted to go to bed now; he was dead tired.

"The caller must have had a name," I tried again, but it was **pointless**. "So what did he want?

---

tension – Spannung;
to be on tenterhooks – gespannt sein;
to crouch down – in der Hocke gehen;
unsure – unsicher;
strict – streng;
pointless – sinnlos

Can you at least remember that? Timmi, you're starting school next year, you're a big boy, and big boys know things like that."

He snuggled into Mum's arms and nodded. "School," he said quietly.

"Maybe he said something about the school party?" Hille helped him out.

Timmi nodded again.

The next question hung in the air: did he say his name was "Alex"? But nobody asked the question. Instead, I made out as if the whole business was a matter of no interest whatsoever to me.

Mum took Timmi to bed and impressed upon me one more time that I had to be home by ten thirty at the latest.

"So? What do you reckon?" I asked Hille who was, in the meantime, mixing two lipsticks together.

"Alex, guaranteed, I can just sense it somehow," she said, viewing her handiwork critically. Then she started giggling. "But this lipstick isn't kiss-proof, you do know that, don't you? Not that I'm going to all this trouble for you to ..."

I hugged her. "Nice of you to explain. I'll **bear it in mind** the whole time. I just hope I'll have a reason to."

---

to bear sth in mind – an etw. denken

As Hille and I were quite early, we stood around undecided outside school for a couple of minutes, wondering whether we should go straight in.

"The really important people always arrive later on in the evening. Around eleven or twelve. That's what I read in the paper recently," said Hille.

She was probably right, but I didn't want to spend long hanging around in the car park while Alex might be enjoying himself with Eileen or Jenny.

"There's just one problem," I countered, "I've got to be back home by half ten. And anyway, there'll be nothing left to eat later on. Did you see the cold buffet they were setting up earlier?"

That convinced Hille. "Come on, then, let's go," she said.

The acting headmistress was just giving a speech in the inner courtyard whilst our school band was setting up its instruments outside the sports hall. A couple of kids from Year Five who were there for the first time applauded when the headmistress declared the school party open.

Hille and I wandered into the sports hall. The music our school band, *DJ Griffin and the Master of Disaster*, was playing was fantastic. That evening I'd dance with Alex and maybe I'd kiss him, too. Well, maybe not kissing so soon, but dancing and holding hands, that simply had to work out.

I looked around surreptitiously. No sign of Alex. Instead we spotted Eileen and Jenny. Hille started **snorting with laughter**.

"Look, Eileen's gone curly! She looks like a metal angel. And as for that dress! Garish green!"

The school band was playing last year's summer hits, and the dance floor was filling up more and more. The entire school seemed to be there. Hille had even spotted a couple of teachers, including Napoleon; only Alex was nowhere to be seen.

"Maybe he'll come later," she said. "Come on, let's dance."

I shook my head. Dancing, so I'd planned, was something I'd only do with *him*. Without me, Hille, of course, didn't dare. Instead she **stuck to me like glue** as I looked at the various stalls the other classes had set up. We joined in a game of skill and bought three **raffle tickets**. Hille won a sandwich box and I won a copy of *Short Instructions for Recorder Players*.

---

to snort with laughter – vor Lachen losprusten;
to stick to sb like glue – wie eine Klette an jmdm. hängen;
raffle ticket – Los

Just as we were about to buy ourselves something to eat, the head boy announced over the loudspeakers that there was to be a surprise that evening – or rather, a sensation.

"Blah, blah, blah," I said to Hille, "that guy's so **shallow**! He'd probably describe there being pasta salad for sale as a sensation."

But I was mistaken. This time he hadn't exaggerated.

"There are 'Miss School' competitions everywhere," he said, "but we're not going to do any of that. The girls at our school don't need it."

The boy was interrupted by enthusiastic howls. He waved them away casually. "We're going to have a 'Mister School' Competition." He raised his voice. "I hereby declare the Georg-Elser-School's first 'Schoolboy-of-the-Year' Competition officially open!"

He left the stage **accompanied** by laughter and resounding applause. A minute later he was back on stage again. Now he seemed slightly embarrassed.

"Um, there's something I forgot! How does it work?" He pulled a piece of paper from his trouser pocket and read aloud. "It's quite simple: those of us in school administration have nominated candidates from practically all years, who because of their almost supernatural good looks – "

Here he was interrupted again by loud howling.

---

shallow – hohl;
to accompany – begleiten

"– who because of their almost supernatural good looks seemed particularly outstanding to us. You all know them. You can see their photos on the wall of pictures which Felicia is about to **unveil**. We've prepared **ballot papers**. So that it all happens democractically and nobody hands in two **votes**, everyone gets a **hand stamp** when they've voted."

Felicia from Year Twelve had meanwhile appeared on the stage. "Every picture has a number, and you just write the corresponding number on your ballot sheet. Okay, so voting isn't compulsory, but we do, of course, hope that you'll all go to cast your vote like good **citizens**. We've lowered the voting age especially for you. You can all vote!"

Everyone started yelling with excitement and streamed to the giant pin board which had meanwhile been set up in front of the stage. It was still covered in white cloth.

"Take your time! Vote for the best-looking, the most charismatic, simply 'the best'!" yelled the lead singer of *DJ Griffin and the Master of Disaster* into the microphone.

I had grabbed Hille by the arm. "Quick, come on, we've got to see this," I cried. "Bet you anything Alex is on it! We absolutely have to vote for him. You'll vote for him, too, won't you?"

---

to unveil – enthüllen;
ballot papers – Stimmzettel;
vote – Wahl;
hand stamp – Stempel auf die Hand;
citizen – Bürger

Hille just nodded. In all the hustle and bustle it was hard to hear even your own words. By **deploying** our elbows to considerable effect, we managed to get to the **partition**. It was still covered.

Four pupils from Year Twelve were standing in front of it and were pulling the cloth aside very gradually whilst the head boy counted: "Three – two – one – zero!" Then we could finally see.

"I don't believe it," someone cried from right at the front. "That has to be a joke." Our sports teacher **bellowed with laughter** next to me. "So whose idea was *that*?" Fixed to the pin board in front of us were ten large-size photos – of pupils from our school, as the head boy kept telling us – except that they were childhood photos.

"Look at that one, number three," laughed Hille next to me. "He's got a dummy in his mouth, and one in each hand. Isn't he sweet? Should we vote for him or for the one with the **stripey babygrow**?"

I turned to her and spotted Alex only a few metres away. Eileen, Jenny and a couple of others from our class were **besieging** him and were presumably trying to get information out of him. I pushed my way through the crowd until I was standing right next to him.

---

to deploy – einsetzen;
partition – Stellwand;
to bellow with laughter – schallend lachen;
stripey – gestreiften; babygrow – Strampelanzug;
to besiege – umlagern

"If you want us to vote for you, you'll have to tell us what number you are," Eileen was saying.

Alex shook his head. "I can't, in fact, even tell you whether I'm one of them. I had to sign a three-page-long **declaration of secrecy**," he **proclaimed**, his face deadly serious. "If I **infringe** it, then I'll be punished by ... erm ..."

"... you'll be punished by Napoleon giving you three History lessons," Carlo helped him out.

Everyone laughed.

"So, you see, I don't have any choice; I have to keep quiet," said Alex. "But I'm sure you'll immediately recognize my charismatic face, so pronounced even in earliest childhood."

We fought our way back through the **cluster** of people in front of the pin board, and I looked at all the photos really carefully.

I'd seen Alex right close up to me so often in my dreams. I knew his eyes, his mouth. It surely had to be quite easy for me to choose the right one. But I wasn't sure. In fact, all the ten little children in the photos looked pretty similar. **Regardless of** whether they were dark-haired or blonde, they all had the same **carefree** expression of children who don't know what life's really like.

---

declaration of secrecy – Geheimhaltungserklärung;
to proclaim – verkünden;
to infringe – verstoßen gegen;
cluster – Menschentraube;
regardless of – ungeachtet;
carefree – unbeschwert

All sorts of wild **conjectures buzzed** through the crowd. "Maybe there are photos of teachers in there," someone said right next to me. "Just imagine: we could vote Maths Maier as Schoolboy of the Year."

After brief consideration I handed in my ballot paper. I had written a big red number seven on it. I was absolutely certain that it was Alex. I'd seen his face in front of me so often in my dreams. I knew every single detail.

"Oh well," said Hille, "you ought to know!" And she wrote a seven on her ballot sheet, too.

At around half nine everyone had voted and the votes were counted by the form leaders. In half an hour, so the head boy declared, we'd know who had won.

In half an hour: then it would already be just after ten, and I was supposed to be home by ten thirty. And I was still absolutely desperate to dance with Alex! I had no choice: I had to ring home and ask my parents to let me stay a bit longer. I'd suggest getting a taxi home and paying for it out of my pocket money. Somehow I'd have to make them see that you can't leave a school party at quarter past ten. That's when it really starts to get interesting.

I looked for Hille so I could borrow her mobile, and found her in the queue for the barbecue. "I've been here for at least ten minutes already, and it

---

conjecture – Vermutung;
to buzz – schwirren

just doesn't move," she groaned. "Do you want me to fetch you a hot dog, too?"

I shook my head. "I just need your phone. I want to ring home and see if I can stay later."

My friend rummaged in her bag. At last, she found her mobile. She stared at the display and shook her head regretfully. "There's no **reception** in the **inner courtyard**. But you can try it outside."

A girl in front of her in the queue **stuck her oar in**. "Try the phone box at the front of the car park. I rang from there last week."

Just to be on the safe side, though, I pocketed Hille's mobile before running off to the car park, The telephone box was empty. I really did seem to be in luck this evening. I picked the receiver up – and immediately **replaced** it, cursing. Some **tosspot** or other had cut the **wire** and had scrawled ***cordless*** *telephone* across the whole apparatus. So I'd have to use Hille's mobile, even if I had to walk for miles to do so.

For a moment I wondered if I should just stay longer without calling my parents, but I didn't want them to worry. In any case, I wouldn't put it past Mum and Dad to appear here at eleven at the latest to fetch me. In front of everyone! Julia's being picked up by her parents like a primary-school kid – I had to spare myself such disgrace.

---

reception – Empfang; inner courtyard – Innenhof;
to stick one's oar in – sich einmischen;
to replace – zurückstellen; tosspot – Depp; wire – Schnur;
cordless – schnurlos

I had no choice but to run around outside, constantly staring at the display in the hope that at some point it would show reasonable reception.

At the back entrance, next to the **wrought-iron** pavilion that the school's **PTA** had founded, it finally worked. Mum answered on the fifth ring.

"Julia, is something wrong? Do you want me to collect you?" she cried when she heard my voice. "Are you still at school? Speak a bit louder. I can hardly hear you!"

I had no desire to yell into the night, but I had no choice. "Please, Mum, it's brilliant here and it's turning really exciting, too, because there's an election going on. Can't I come home later?"

Mum seemed to think briefly. "Okay, you can come home quarter of an hour later."

Quarter of an hour! Don't make me laugh!

"I'll pay for the taxi," I cried, "half eleven, okay?"

"Julia, you're still a child," said Mum.

I could have wept. When would my parents finally realize that I was almost grown up? When it came to household cleaning duties, they certainly didn't treat me as a child.

I **gave a start**. Something had moved in the pavilion. A big dark figure was sitting there. Suddenly it stood up and came directly towards me. I

---

wrought-iron – schmiedeeisern;
PTA (Parent Teacher's Association) – Elternbeirat, Förderverein;
to give a start – zusammenzucken

was **gripped** by **fear**. For a moment I was as if **paralysed**. Only when he was standing right in front of me, did I recognize him.

Alex!

He smiled at me and gesticulated. **I didn't have a clue** what he was on about.

"What's going on?" I heard Mum calling down the phone. "Are you still there? Hello? Hello?"

I'd finally **got it**.

Alex took the mobile from me and grinned at me. "Yes, good evening," he said, "I'm Julia's Maths teacher. Maybe you should allow your daughter to stay a bit longer after all. It's obviously good for the community spirit in the class if everyone's here this evening. She's the only one who has to leave early."

He listened to Mum's torrent of words as I stood there at a loss, just watching. Alex was simply fantastic! A born actor.

He was still grinning as he gave me the phone back again. "Your mother wants to say something else to you," he said.

"I had no idea you had a male Maths teacher," Mum said.

"He's new," I told her. "We'll probably get him next school year. He's really nice."

"His voice sounds very young," said my moth-

---

to grip – greifen, packen;
fear – Angst; paralysed – gelähmt;
I didn't have a clue – ich hatte keine Ahnung;
to get it – verstehen

er. "But what he said is right. So you can stay until half eleven, but then that's it – understood? There won't be any more **extensions**. And make sure you take a taxi. We'll pay."

I promised to take a taxi, one hundred percent, and ended the call.

Alex stood in front of me, just looking. Neither of us said a word. It should in fact have been a mild night with a full moon, a silky black sky and twinkling stars. Instead we had a half moon, it was cloudy, and a cool puff of wind swept round the walls now and then. But none of that bothered me in the slightest; I simply felt **insanely** happy.

Alex had crouched down next to the pavilion and was staring into the night. I sat down really close to him. Just days ago I would have found it difficult, but now it was suddenly quite easy. "Hey, Alex, I really like you," I said, and my voice didn't tremble **in the slightest**.

He turned his head briefly. "I like you, too. At least you're not as **irritating** as Jenny or Eileen. You're just really nice. I've thought so right from the start."

"What are you actually doing here?" I asked quietly. "Why aren't you over there at the party?"

"I had to be on my own for a bit, to think about all the stuff that's going round my head. The others and all the noise just **got on my nerves**."

---

extension – Verlängerung; insanely – wahnsinnig;
not in the slightest – nicht im Geringsten;
to irritate – nerven; to get on sb's nerves – jmdn. nerven

He carefully plucked a daisy and then stared into the night again. Distant music could be heard coming from the school's inner courtyard. A fanfare resounded. They were probably about to announce who was Schoolboy of the Year. But none of that was of any interest to me now; the only thing that mattered was that Alex and I had found one another.

I leaned against him and he put his arm around me. For a moment I felt quite dizzy. If only Eileen and Jenny and the others could see us! Julia, who'd never been the star of the class, is sitting with Alex, the total king, in front of the pavilion, and he's got his arm round her. I desperately needed to preserve this feeling in my diary immediately.

I fell in love with you that time when you had to sit next to me in Napoleon's History lesson, I wanted to say, and I wanted to tell him about my dream. But something about the way he looked made me feel unsure. I was so close to my goal – but what now?

Alex pulled a closely-written piece of paper out of his trouser pocket. "I want to read you something. I wrote it yesterday.

Darling!
Whatever may happen
I'll wait for you.
Every day
Every night

---

darling – Liebling

Always!
Nothing on earth will part us
Nothing anywhere.
Love ***binds*** *us*
Deeper than the ocean
That can't keep us apart."

He grinned, embarrassed. "Oh well. It's a bit like the poem I wrote for the school newspaper. But I think it's even better than that one. Do you like it?"

"Did you write that yourself?" I could barely believe it. Alex writes this amazing poem for me, full of feeling and stuff. Compared to that, Hille's appearance in the *Farmers' Weekly* was nothing.

I reached out for the piece of paper, but Alex shook his head. "I don't know whether she'll even want me showing the poem to anyone else. I just did it because ..." He shrugged his shoulders and seemed rather embarrassed again. "You've got a really strange look. Don't tell anyone about the poem, promise? Even Hille. The others would just laugh themselves silly if they heard that I was writing poems for my girlfriend."

I felt the ground being pulled away from under my feet. I felt as I'd felt once at a party when I'd opened a present that wasn't for me at all, but for another child. Then all the adults had laughed as I forced the present into the other girl's hands and ran out of the room, angry, hurt, sad.

---

to bind – verbinden

Alex hadn't written the poem for me; that much was clear.

"Lindsay's coming to Germany next month," he said. "I should think you'd get on brilliantly. She's a great girl, like you." He gave me a gentle punch on the upper arm. "If I didn't know her, I'd have fallen straight in love with *you*."

If, if, if ... I waited to feel that pain that I'd have to feel when Alex, whom I was so madly in love with, told me about his girlfriend. But I didn't feel anything! Absolutely nothing! A bit disappointed, perhaps, but I wasn't angry, I wasn't sad, and I wasn't hurt. Maybe relieved, in fact?

I stood up. "Come on, let's go back over," I suggested. "I want to know who won the competition. So what number are you, then?"

He shook his head. "I signed that secrecy clause. Oh well, I'll make an exception and tell you if you tell me first who you voted for."

"Seven. I'm sure you're number seven."

He pulled a mock sad face. "You didn't recognize me either. But I'm giving nothing away. Hakan and Carlo persuaded me to join in. The boys in the upper school don't dare. In the end, five kids from our class, two from Year Six, one from Year Eight, and one from Year Five did it. Or the other way round; I don't remember it that well any more."

I had counted with him. "That's nine. So who's the tenth?"

Alex grinned conspiratorially. "That's Mr X. I can't say. All I can tell you is that it was hideously difficult to put the picture together. We had to work a fair bit of magic on the computer to make sure everything on the picture fitted in."

"Come on, tell me!"

But Alex steadfastly **refused**. He could tell me anything, he said, but he would not **disclose** this secret.

He had put his arm around me as we entered the inner courtyard. I looked at the clock: twenty past ten. They didn't seem to have finished counting the ballot papers yet.

I looked around for Hille and the others in my class. They should just all see how well Alex and I got on together.

"There they are, sitting back there!" Alex pointed to a table not far from the **grandstand**, where Carlo and Rita were sitting. "Shall we sit with them and have something to eat? Not a word to the others about Lindsay, okay?"

I nodded. Alex and I got on well together. I was the only one he took into his confidence, perhaps precisely because he wasn't in love with me. I suddenly felt quite relieved. Light-hearted, simply carefree. Holding hands with Alex, I ran over to the others.

"So where have you been?" Eileen looked a bit fed up when she saw us. "Do you want to come and sit with us? There's not much room here." Her eyes almost popped out of her head when she saw

---

to refuse – ablehnen; to disclose – lüften;
grandstand – Tribüne

that we were holding hands, but she acted pretty cool.

"Of course, there's room!" Hille was talking with her mouth full again. "We'll just budge up a bit, and if Julia squeezes in next to me, then it's fine." She turned to Eileen. "You always have to make such a drama out of everything!"

Eileen just said she didn't want to sit around any longer anyway, and that she'd **rather** go and dance. She pushed off with Jenny and Rita in tow.

"Brilliant," Hille whispered to me when Alex went off to fetch the drinks. "Everything's **sorted** between you, is it?"

"Everything's sorted, but not in the way I planned," I said quietly. "I'll tell you later. It's an amazing story."

I smiled at Carlo, who was sitting directly opposite me. I'd not exchanged a single word with him all evening. "Who's Schoolboy of the Year?" I asked him. "Or aren't the results out yet?"

"They'd got to that stage before, but then it turned out that they'd forgotten at least 30 ballot papers, so just the usual chaos." Carlo's voice sounded **calm**, but I could sense an undertone.

Was he sad? Was he having trouble at home again? I looked into his eyes searchingly, but he turned away.

"We've done it," the head boy cried down the

---

rather – lieber;
to be sorted – klar sein;
calm – ruhig

microphone at that point. "Our vote has been successfully **concluded**. We have – and our politicians could **take a leaf out of our book** – achieved a turnout of 100 percent!"

Cue enthusiastic applause.

"Before we disclose the secret of who is the winner and who may be crowned with the title of Schoolboy of the Year for the whole year, we want to reveal who's behind the pictures. I ask Number One to come up on stage!"

A **lanky** boy from Year Six trotted up onto the stage, accompanied by applause from his classmates. He received a certificate from the head boy, which he **raised** triumphantly in the air.

The head boy called out the names of the **participants** one at a time and announced how many votes they had received each time. He left out only number three.

"Number seven," he called at last. "Where's number seven?"

I turned inquiringly to Alex, but he just shook his head and grinned. "Wrong," he said. "There's number seven!"

Carlo stood up. He smiled at me before going up to the front.

Hille grabbed my arm. "Hey, I don't get it. Carlo! And you were absolutely sure that it was Alex. Hey,

---

to conclude – beenden; to take a leaf out of our book – an uns ein Beispiel nehmen;
cue – Einsatz; lanky – schlaksig;
to raise – erheben;
participant – Teilnehmer

is something wrong, Julia? You've got such a funny look!"

I shook my head. Of course, the baby photo was of Carlo. That's why the face was so well-known to me, so **familiar**. Only I'd reckoned on it being Alex!

Alex was number nine. He stood next to Carlo, waving, and put his arm round him. "Our dream team," cried the head boy, and then he paused significantly.

"And now we come to our winner, to whom we, of course, offer a prize. It consists of three free Maths lessons with our dear Frau Frederici." A few pupils booed loudly, but most **clapped** like mad.

"Schoolboy of the Year, with 86 votes, is Number Three!" The head boy was **croaking** hoarsely. "But before you all start complaining, I have to tell you that it's all your own **fault**. At the end of the day, you chose him. And the winner of today's competition is" – his voice almost cracked – "our Herr Dieringer, also known affectionately as Napoleon."

The band played a fanfare and Napoleon grabbed the microphone, grinning **broadly**.

"Thank you for your vote of confidence. I hope I shall **prove** a worthy **representative** of our school in all the competitions on the agenda –

---

familiar – bekannt;
to clap – klatschen; to croak – krächzen;
fault – Schuld; broadly – breit;
to prove – beweisen;
representative – Vertreter

beauty and otherwise. I should also like to thank the computer freaks who so professionally created this unusual photo montage." He pointed to the photo of himself sitting on a child's car in short Lederhosen. "I am, of course, particularly delighted by the extraordinarily tasteful prize which you have given me: three Maths lessons with Frau Frederici! I can hardly bring myself to accept it!"

"Fantastic!" Hille and I exchanged looks. Napoleon was showing a human side. He could even manage quite a friendly grin, not just the revolting one he used during class.

Carlo and Alex returned to our table. Alex was carrying two bowls of pasta salad.

"It's all they had left," he said apologetically as he put one of the plates in front of me. "What's more, I'm afraid it's not going to be particularly tasty." He leaned over to me. "Lindsay makes the best pasta salad in the whole of America. When she comes, we'll invite you for one."

But I thought the pasta salad tasted great. The mood I was in, I could probably have eaten worms with tomato sauce and thought it was delicious.

I stood up and laughed at Alex. "Shall we dance?"

I was pretty sure that Eileen and Jenny and various others would have wished me anywhere but there when I went off to the dance floor with Alex. I could positively read their minds. The absolute star of the school was dancing with Julia. Why on earth with her and not with Eileen? Even a blind person could see that Alex and Julia got on well together.

"I can't wait to meet Lindsay," I called to Alex.

He said, "Shh, it's still a secret," but with all the noise that was going on around us, there's no way anyone could have heard.

DJ Griffin and the Master of Disaster were playing a slow number. "Then that's it," the lead singer had announced, "that's definitively it: otherwise we'll get into trouble with the **local residents**, and in any case you've all got to go to bed like good kids."

"So?" asked Alex after the first couple of **bars**. "Do you like this music?" He pulled me really close to him, just as I'd wanted him to do. "Come on," he whispered, holding me **gently** by the **chin**. "Come on!"

In the semi-darkness I could see Eileen, Jenny and a couple of others from my class standing at the side of the dance floor. They were all staring at us.

It seemed to me as if the music was getting louder and louder, as if everything around me was spinning. Alex's face was quite close to me, any minute now he'd kiss me. Carlo was somewhere in the crowd, looking in our direction.

"No!" I suddenly heard myself saying. "Alex, it was all just a mistake!"

He laughed. "Okay, that's fine. I thought you wanted me to kiss you!"

---

local resident – Anwohner; bar – Takt;
gently – sanft; chin – Kinn

I shook my head. Alex, I could have said, I did want you to a couple of days ago, but since then …

I suddenly didn't know myself exactly what was going on. The main thing, however, was that I thought that Alex was nice and funny, but no more than that.

"I absolutely have to go and dance with Eileen and Jenny, or they'll be angry with me," he said once the song had finished and the lead singer was announcing the 'absolutely last encore of the evening'.

"Shall we see each other afterwards?"

"Maybe," I said.

I wanted to be alone so I could think about what had happened. Why had the feelings I'd had for Alex disappeared so suddenly? Was it just because I'd found out about Lindsay?

No, I had to admit to myself. I had suddenly seen that the real Alex wasn't at all like the one I'd thought was so fantastic in my dreams. In fact, he was pretty childish: he liked reading comics, fooled around and didn't seem to take anything or anyone seriously.

"Julia, I'm going now!" Hille had spotted me and was waving to me. "I'm starting to get pretty **chilly** and … are you coming? Are you finally going to tell me what's actually going on between you and Alex?"

I nodded.

The weather had finally changed. It had turned

---

chilly – kalt

cool, and all around us people were clearing up. I fetched my jacket and waved to Alex and Eileen. He had put his arm round her and gave me a conspiratorial grin. I grinned back as I made my way to the car park with Hille.

"So, out with it at last," nagged my friend. "Why's he suddenly hanging around with Eileen? I really just don't get any of this."

But I didn't get round to it.

"You can't just leave," someone behind us cried. "Who do you think's going to do all the work?"

I turned round and saw Frau Frederici shifting desks with Napoleon.

"Don't worry, I'll give you a lift home afterwards," she said. "But you surely realize that you can't just leave a party without at least offering to help with the **clearing up**."

"Hille and Rita, you get the cutlery from the tables, Alex and Albert can stack the tables, and Julia and ..." Frederici looked around to see if she could see any more helpers, "... and Carlo, you two can load the dishwasher."

The school management had hired a gigantic dishwasher for the evening, and it had to be filled up. This year, you see, we hadn't used plastic cutlery for environmental reasons. Carlo handed me the plates and glasses and I stacked the cutlery in the dishwasher. Neither of us said a word.

I suddenly felt **awkward**. What on earth was

---

clearing up – Aufräumen; awkward – befangen

going on between Carlo and me? Why couldn't we talk as we used to?

"Watch it, that glass is broken!"

I looked up. Our hands touched as he carefully took the glass out of my hand. He was standing quite close to me.

I was wrong, I thought, he hasn't got grey-blue eyes at all. Carlo's eyes are dark blue, as dark as … I couldn't think of a **suitable comparison**. I wanted to look away, but I just couldn't.

"Julia?"

We were still looking into one another's eyes.

He had turned slightly red. "I wanted to ask you something …" He **chewed** his lower lip. "You and Alex …?"

I shook my head. "I thought for quite a while that I was in love with him," I said quietly. "But in reality we're just friends. In any case, he's already got a girlfriend."

Carlo smiled. It occurred to me that he'd changed quite a lot recently. He seemed more **mature**, more adult than the Carlo I thought I knew.

"By the way, I rang you this evening," he said. "I wanted to ask if you'd go to the school party with me."

Someone had opened the window wide. We could hear faint rumblings of thunder in the dis-

---

suitable – passend;
comparison – Vergleich;
to chew – kauen;
mature – reif

tance. We stood by the window and watched the mountains of cloud scudding by. We were standing really close to one another. Suddenly I saw everything more clearly than ever before in my life.

The truth is that I'm in love with Carlo and I failed to notice it the whole time, I thought. It's totally insane. Suddenly I could have wept with happiness.

"I like walking through the rain," I said after a while.

Carlo nodded. "Come on, let's go!"

I **cast one last look** at the half-cleared-up school kitchen. Frederici was issuing orders somewhere; someone dropped a bottle; I could hear Alex and Eileen laughing loudly.

I looked at Carlo. He smiled.

The first drops of rain started to fall outside. He took my hand and we ran into the open air.

---

to cast a look – ein Blick werfen

Bei Thienemann u. a. bereits erschienen:

Sabine Both: *Move to Cloud Nine*
Brinx/Kömmerling: *A Paul to Kiss*
Christamaria Fiedler: *Spaghetti Crime*
Sissi Flegel: *Forbidden to Love*
Bianka Minte-König: *Mobile Phone Love, Schoolyard Flirt & Catwalk Dreams*
Hortense Ullrich: *Love is Blonde*
Hortense Ullrich: *Never Kiss a Witch*
Zimmermann & Zimmermann:
Maths, Stress & a Lovesick Heart
Summer, Sun & Holiday Love

Zimmermann, Irene:
School, Trouble & True Love
Aus dem Deutschen von Helena Ragg-Kirkby
ISBN 978 3 522 17807 5

Reihengestaltung: Birgit Schössow
Einbandillustration: Birgit Schössow
Texttypografie: Marlis Killermann
Schrift: Stone serif und Spumoni
Satz: KCS GmbH, Buchholz/Hamburg
Reproduktion: Medienfabrik, Möglingen
Druck und Bindung: Friedrich Pustet, Regensburg

6 5 4 3 2* 07 08 09 10

www.thienemann.de
www.frechemaedchen.de